A TYPICAL GORGE IN THE SARHAD.

THE RAIDERS OF THE SARHAD

BEING THE ACCOUNT OF A CAMPAIGN OF ARMS AND BLUFF AGAINST THE BRIGANDS OF THE PERSIAN-BALUCHI BORDER DURING THE GREAT WAR

BY
BRIGADIER-GENERAL R. E. H. DYER, C.B.

WITH NUMEROUS PHOTOGRAPHS AND TWO MAPS

The Naval & Military Press Ltd

Published and © by the
The Naval & Military Press

Unit 10 Ridgewood Industrial Park,
Uckfield, East Sussex, TN22 5QE
Tel: +44 (0) 1825 749494
Fax: +44 (0) 1825 765701

Printed and bound in Great Britain by
CPI Antony Rowe, Chippenham and Eastbourne

In reprinting in facsimile from the original, any imperfections are inevitably reproduced and the quality may fall short of modern type and cartographic standards.

PREFACE

WITH the greatest diffidence I have at last made up my mind to write the story of my small campaign with the Sarhad Raiders in 1916.

This campaign sinks into utter insignificance when compared with the great deeds done in other theatres of war by men who said nothing about them. But, insignificant as it was, it forms part of the mosaic of the Great War, and for this reason may be of some general interest.

I take this opportunity of paying a tribute to all the officers who took part in this little campaign. Their untiring devotion to duty, and their efforts to do their utmost under conditions that were often more than trying, accounts for its success.

I would like, in particular, to mention Major Landon of the 35th Scinde Horse, whose great knowledge of the people and their country was invaluable; Major Sanders of the 36th Sikhs; Colonel Claridge of the 28th Light Cavalry; Captain Brownlow and Captain Hirst, both of the 28th Light Cavalry; Major Lang; Captain Moore-

Lane; Lieutenant Bream of the Hazara Pioneers, and Captain English, R.A.

In addition I would mention how much, not only I, but the old country owes to Khan Bahadur, the Sarhad-dar, and to Idu, non-commissioned officer of the Chagai Levies.

The photographs are from snapshots taken by various officers during the campaign.

R.E.H.D.

CONTENTS

CHAPTER I

ORDERS FOR THE WEST

CHAPTER II

THE ROAD TO ROBAT

CHAPTER III

A PLAN OF CAMPAIGN

CONTENTS

CHAPTER VIII

KHWASH AND THE SECOND SURRENDER

CHAPTER IX

TREACHERY AND ITS SEQUEL

CHAPTER X

FAILURE AND FRESH PLANS

CHAPTER XI

SUCCESS IN MINIATURE

CHAPTER XII

VICTORY AND PEACE

LIST OF ILLUSTRATIONS

MAPS

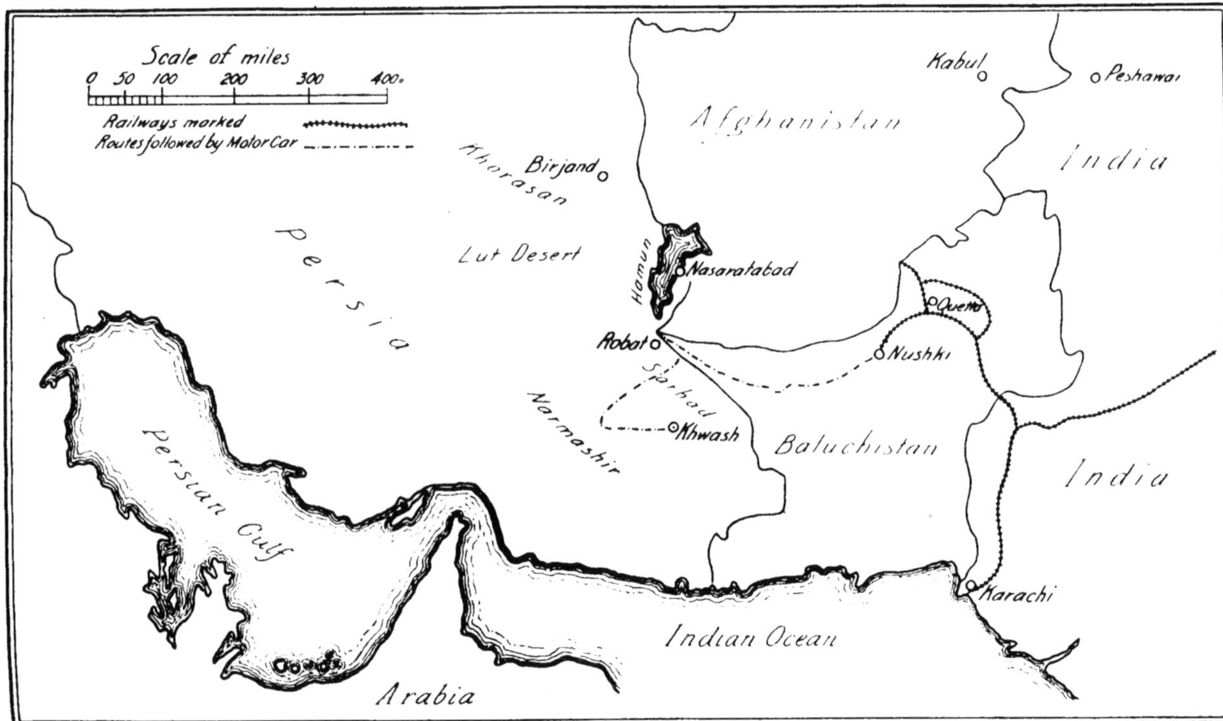

Sketch Map of the Persian-Baluchi Afghan frontiers

THE RAIDERS OF THE SARHAD

CHAPTER I

ORDERS FOR THE WEST

I receive my orders—German agents and India—Their routes—A deal in chauffeurs—Concerning an appetite and sausages—Nushliki—The last of civilisation—Further information—Sand-holes and digging—Petrol in the desert.

TOWARDS the end of February, 1916, General Kirkpatrick, Chief of Staff at Delhi, sent for me and gave me orders to take charge of the military operations in South-East Persia.

Although Persia, as a country, was neutral during the War, there is a certain district in the South-East, abutting on to the frontiers of Afghanistan and of Baluchistan, and known as the Sarhad, which is occupied by a number of nomad tribes who claim absolute independence. At this time these tribes were causing considerable embarrassment and difficulty to the Indian Government.

The Germans and their agents, who were past masters in the art of propaganda, were still endeavouring, as they had done for years before the outbreak of hostilities, to work upon the discontented portion of the Indian population in the hope of rousing them into open rebellion. They believed this to be quite possible, in spite of the magnificent way in which India had offered her resources of men and money to the British Raj, and hoped thereby to handicap us still further in our great struggle in the West.

They were pouring their agents, with their lying propaganda, into India via Persia and Afghanistan. Afghanistan, like Persia, was nominally neutral, but she was breaking her neutrality by many open acts of aggression, and was offering every facility in her power to the German agents in their passage through her territories, and thence into the Punjab.

To reach Afghanistan, however, the German agents had to pass through some part of Persia. The Persian Government placed no restrictions on the movements of either British or Germans, of which fact the latter took full advantage.

A glance at the map will show that apparently the easiest route for them to take across Persia was in the North, in the Russian sphere of influence, and to approach Afghanistan through Korasan; or, failing this, by a route rather farther South, across the Lut Desert, in the direction of Birjand. As a matter of fact they had tried both these routes, but without much success, owing to the inhospitable nature of the country through which they had to pass and also to the opposition they met with from the Hazara tribes round Herat, who, belonging as they do to the Shiah section of the Mahommedan religion, are at daggers drawn with the Afghans, who belong to the Sunni section.

Therefore the Germans had to try yet another road, and succeeded farther South where they had failed in the North. By taking the longer route through Kerman and Narmashir in the South and South-East of Persia, they found easy ingress into Afghanistan.

To effect this, however, they had to make friends with the nomad and war-like tribes of the Sarhad. These tribes were traditionally friendly to the British, but the Germans had bribed them heavily and had moreover assured them that Germany had turned Islam and that the Kaiser William himself was a convert to their religion. As the Sarhad tribes were always out for a good thing for themselves, and as they believed the lie about the German conversion, they had allowed themselves to be tricked into helping the Germans. This they were doing not only by permitting them to pass through their territory, but also by harassing the lines of communication between the inadequately small British frontier posts.

The story of Germany having turned Mahommedan, farcical as it was, was nevertheless a potential source of grave danger for us in India. It must be remembered that Germany's ally, Turkey, was Mahommedan, and that in helping us against Germany, the Mahommedans of India were already being called upon, indirectly, to fight against their own co-religionists. When, in addition, India was assured that powerful Germany was winning, so her agents avowed, in every theatre of war, it was inevitable that in time her loyalty to us must suffer.

It was vital to stop this lying but insidious propaganda, and the first step was to prevent German agents from entering India at all. To do this the nomad tribes of the Sarhad must be brought back into line with their old policy of friendship with Britain. Hence my orders from General Kirkpatrick.

He instructed me to proceed without a moment's unnecessary delay to Quetta, where I was to receive more detailed instructions.

On leaving him I hurried, with car and native chauffeur, to the railway station, and asked for a truck on which to place the car for entrainment to Nushki. The station-master assured me I was asking for an impossibility. A great Maharajah, then travelling, had commandeered every available truck for his suite, luggage and cars. I told him that the Government business on which I had been sent was all important, and, by a little persuasion, soon had myself on the way to Pindi and the car on the way to Nushki.

Arrived at Pindi I found I had exactly one hour left in which to catch the train for Quetta. There was no time to pack, sort out kit, or decide what should, or should not, be taken on a campaign which might last only a few weeks or many months, and which might assume a political aspect sooner than expected. My servant, Allah-dad, was therefore directed to take everything for sorting out when time could be spared, and I rushed off to try and "do a deal" with General Sir Gerald Kitson, before starting.

I realised that a motor-car might play an important part in this prospective campaign, as it would be necessary to travel for long distances in a land of no railways and no regular roads, the best road to be hoped for probably being a sandy track used by camel caravans. I had already had some experience of difficult motoring with an inefficient chauffeur, so naturally wanted to secure the best man that could be got.

I must here explain that I possessed an English chauffeur, Allan by name, and that General Kitson employed his brother in the same capacity. Now, without any disparagement of *my* Allan, I knew his brother to be a more practical and experienced man. General Kitson generously gave his consent to an exchange of chauffeurs.

I may as well say, at once, that it was a lucky day for me that saw Allan of the 9th Middlesex Regiment enter my service, for, during the months to come, he was as cheery and full of resource as he was ready for any event, however untoward. His appetite stood forth as the only thing that ever caused me uneasiness, and I must admit that I have never met a man with one of such colossal proportion. As an instance—on one occasion, when camped out in the desert, between Nushki and Robat, and supplies were none too plentiful, we cooked twelve sausages for breakfast.

I had one, and then was persuaded by Allan to attempt a second. I only succeeded in disposing of half of it. I then got up and left Allan to have his own breakfast. Allah-dad, being a Mahommedan, of course refused to touch sausage.

At lunch-time Allah-dad asked what I would have to eat, and got the answer, " Oh, some of the cold sausages left from breakfast."

Allah-dad replied, " But there are no sausages, Sahib. Allan has eaten them all."

I expostulated, maintaining that it was impossible. No normal man could have eaten ten and a half large sausages. But Allah-dad was not to be shaken. It may be well imagined that the feeding of my chauffeur during the months to come loomed up as one of my minor anxieties.

From Pindi I went to Quetta by train, my car, with the native chauffeur having gone direct to the then rail-head at Nushki, in the North of Indo-Baluchistan.

At Quetta I laid in a store of petrol, spare tyres, a few personal necessities, reported to General Grover for orders and information, and then proceeded to Nushki; which place was reached, and the car picked up, on, if I remember rightly, the 25th of February.

This day in Nushki was to prove the last in a civilised town for many months to come. The look of the country lying before us so intimidated my native chauffeur that he came to me, a short time before we were due to start, with a countenance torn with grief and, with lamentations and protestations of sorrow, told me that both his father and mother were ill, and that it was vital for him to return and succour them. As I had been in two minds as to the advisability of taking the rascal with me, this sign of the white feather at the very outset at once decided the point, and I gave him to understand that he could go and bury as many of his relations as he pleased. With a countenance swiftly transformed to cheerfulness he left me.

Just before starting a wire was handed in from a high political official at Quetta informing me that the Baluch Raiders had already cut our lines of communication, were right across my path, and he advised, if not ordered, me not to proceed.

However, as explicit military instructions were to endeavour to reach Robat (near the Koh-i-Maliksia), a hill at which the Baluch, Afghan and Persian frontiers meet, as well as that of the district known as the Sarhad, with the least possible delay, and as I knew the Raiders were across my path even before I left Quetta, I saw no reason for altering previously made plans or for delaying my departure.

Accordingly I started on the journey to Robat early on the morning of the 27th. I reckoned it would take at least five days to reach that town, as the route it would be necessary to follow would be fully three hundred and seventy-five miles. I already knew that it would be essential to make many long détours round freshly formed sand dunes and other obstacles, for it must be remembered that there was no proper road but only a rough camel-track continually blown over and obliterated by sand, along which supplies were taken from India to Robat, and the small garrison posts which we had established at various points Northward.

The mention of small garrison posts may lead the reader to suppose that this area of wild activity was fairly well policed, but, as a fact, one battalion of Indian infantry, a regiment of Indian cavalry and, I believe, four mountain guns, constituted the entire force of regulars holding a front of close upon three hundred miles. It was small wonder, then, that the Sarhad tribes, commonly known as Raiders, from their raiding proclivities, who knew every inch of the country, could climb like cats, and could do long marches on short rations, had succeeded in cutting our lines of communication, and in carrying off our supplies.

I could, therefore, look for no further help for the time in the matter of supplies and so took with me all that I thought would be necessary for our three hundred and seventy-five mile trek across the sandy wastes lying between Nushki and Robat.

Petrol was, at the moment, the most important of

our needs; we had, therefore, to carry with us all we should require, making allowance at the same time for mishaps. Moreover, we had to take enough food and water to last Allan, Allah-dad and myself for five or six days.

As regards personal luggage we travelled absolutely light, leaving all kit to follow at a slower pace on camels, together with my horse, Galahad. I had some compunction in leaving the latter behind, but my orders were concise and urgent—to reach Robat, endeavour to get into touch with all our scattered posts, and effect a combination against the Raiders at the earliest possible moment.

A start was made very early in the morning, but the first day's journey proved disappointing. Instead of doing the ninety miles planned, we only accomplished thirty. The track was even worse than I had expected, for we constantly ran into sand-hills, and had to dig the car out. I have never done so much digging in my life as I did on that journey to Robat. Sand-hills were, however, only a portion of our afflictions, for, in addition, there were many water pools and small shallow lakes—due to recent rain—which had to be taken at a rush, or somehow circumvented.

So serious, at last, did our rate of progress become that, as we approached what seemed to be the hundredth of these wide, shallow pools, I lost patience and ordered Allan to drive straight through.

He attempted to carry out the order, but about

half-way we sank up to the axle and stuck. No power on earth would induce the car to budge another inch, and, though we all three got out into the water, and lugged, pushed and dragged at the wretched car, no impression could be made upon her.

So we remained till, at last, about two a.m., I caught sight of a light on a small hill not very far away in the west, and, on going over to it, found a sort of recluse, or holy man, quietly cooking his food. After the usual courtesies I asked him to come and help me to pull my car out. He replied that he was an old man and could not do much by himself, but that a caravan of nomads, who had arrived the evening before, were encamped close by. So off I went again, flushed my " quarry," and, with the help of large bribes, persuaded all the able-bodied men to come back to the car. Fortunately we carried a good strong rope as part of our kit, so soon had the car out and running again.

Allan was never again ordered to drive through water on that route.

On the second day our troubles recommenced, for we had barely done a dozen miles than we stuck in another sand-hill, and the laborious digging-out process had to be done all over again. Fortunately, the party who had got the car out of the lake the night before were close behind, and for an obvious reason. They had been given so many rupees for their timely help that, knowing the difficulties lying ahead, they had followed in the hope of further largesse. They got it.

Once safely out again I made a tour of inspection round the car, but only to find more trouble.

" Hullo, what on earth is this, Allan? She's leaking! "

Allan smiled a superior smile. " I don't think so, sir. My cars don't leak."

But a moment later his superiority turned to consternation, and he was burying his head in the bowels of the car.

After a moment's inspection he showed a face of such utter dismay that it would have been comical had not the situation been so serious.

" Great Scott, sir! I must have left the petrol tap turned on, and the tank is nearly empty."

Here, I'm afraid, my language was violent, and it was some minutes before Allan was able to ascertain exactly how much petrol we had left. His calculations established the fact that we had lost some fourteen gallons. This meant that we should have to walk the greater part of the last two hundred miles of our journey. A pleasant prospect in that forbidding country. But orders were to go on, and go on we did.

That day we made good time, and before evening had done the ninety miles set as a day's march. But, as we had lost so much ground the previous day, I determined to go on as long as Allan could stick at the driving wheel, and we went on—to a post called Yadgar.

I should explain that in this barren, townless, roadless district there are occasional small rest-houses, very modest types of Dâk bungalows, established by the Indian Government for the benefit of travellers, or soldiers on their way to frontier duty. They are quite bare except for a camp bed or two, a tub, a table, a few chairs and a wash-hand basin, with a *chokidar*, or keeper, in charge.

Such a rest-house we found at Yadgar, and being not only very tired and dusty, but filthily dirty, as the result of our struggles with the car, we pulled up to try and get a superficial wash.

I jumped out and tried the door. It was locked, and I banged loudly without getting any answer. It would not do to lose an unnecessary minute, for the many miles we should have to walk later on loomed unpleasantly ahead, but I knew there were pretty certain to be water and washing-basin behind that door, and did not intend to leave them unused if I could help it, *chokidar* or no *chokidar*. So, I took a butting run with my shoulder, the door gave, and I set out in search of the water tub.

An open door on my right showed me a small room, absolutely empty, except for a row of tins against the wall. Knowing that petrol was carried in such tin drums I went and examined them. The next moment Allan heard a shout that brought him hastily inside, wondering whether I had gone mad, had been bitten by a wild beast, or was being murdered.

" Look! " I cried, as he came running up to me. " Look at those tins and tell me what's inside! "

Allan seized hold of one of the drums, read what was written on it, gave it a shake, and we could both hear the blessed sound of lapping inside.

" It's petrol, sir," he whispered in an awed voice.

Petrol in the desert—petrol where one would as soon have expected to find a Bond Street jeweller!

At first we could neither of us believe it. Personally I imagined we had both got temporary jim-jams, but Allan, with his usual stolid, common sense, opened one of the drums, tested the contents, and pronounced it to be first-class petrol. There were seven drums, each containing four gallons.

" This means we'll motor, not walk into Robat after all, sir," said Allan, with a grin and sigh of relief. The thought of those miles of desert—nearly two hundred of them—which confronted us after the mishap had been haunting us both like a nightmare.

At this moment the *chokidar* returned, in great trepidation, fearing a dressing-down for being absent from duty. But I was far too elated at the turn of events to want to swear at anyone.

I asked him where the petrol had come from, and whose it was. He shook his head, and said he had no idea. It had always been there. It belonged to no one, and no one had put it there, so far as he knew. He had never seen a car there before; in fact, he had never seen a car anywhere before, and could not understand how it was that men could travel on a thing which was not alive, which was not like any horse or camel he had ever seen.

This was all very good hearing, so I proceeded to tell him that the petrol belonged to me, and, as he quite cheerfully acquiesced, I gave him a receipt which he could show to any Government official in case of needed absolution in the future. As we now had means to finish our journey by car, I decided to spend the night at the rest-house.

After a simple camp meal Allan, worn out with the strenuous work of the past two days and night, was quickly snoring in the deep sleep of exhaustion, so I went for a stroll.

As I paced up and down I tried to draw up some preliminary plan for the coming campaign. But such occupation was somewhat futile, as, until I could reach Robat, I had no knowledge at all as to the strength and composition of the force that would be at my disposal. But upon one thing I made up my mind—even at that early stage—I would do my utmost to show these Raiders, who were doing us so much harm, that they could not do this with impunity. The lesson once driven home, an endeavour should be made to become friendly with them, to win them back to our side, and, so to speak, appoint them as doorkeepers of the Baluchistan frontier; but doorkeepers with their rifles pointed at our enemies instead of at ourselves.

In the midst of these meditations I found myself stumbling with fatigue, so, with a last look at the beauty of the night, I turned indoors, and in a few minutes was sound asleep, and making up for the " whiteness " of the night before.

CHAPTER II

THE ROAD TO ROBAT

Mushki-chah—The native contractor—An evening rencontre—Idu of the Chagai Levies—The native idea of an airship—Idu the invaluable—Robat.

On the third day we made good progress, fate being kind in helping us to avoid the sandy pitfalls which had hitherto been our undoing, and, by nightfall, we found ourselves approaching the post of Mushki-chah.

Here we found the road blocked with a number of camel caravans carrying Government food supplies for our scattered posts along the frontier. These posts were already in difficulties owing to the Raiders' interference with their commissariat.

As can be imagined there was a great deal of noise, the native drivers gesticulating and talking in a way which proved that something was afoot. I got out of the car and asked who was in charge of the caravan. A huge native contractor was pointed out to me, and, summoning him to my side I asked him what all the hubbub was about.

He was in a state of great agitation and told me that he had received information from several reliable sources that the whole of the countryside ahead of them was in the hands of the Raiders, and that, therefore, it was useless to go a step further.

I expostulated with the man, pointing out that, by the terms of his contract, he must go on, and that if he did not the soldiers for whom he was bringing supplies would die of starvation.

But he was dogged. He knew too well the methods of the Raiders with the men they captured.

" It's no use, Sahib," he said, respectfully but firmly. " My men will not go on as they are unarmed, and a single armed Raider is enough to hold up the whole caravan."

I knew the man was right, but persisted in my efforts to persuade him to chance it, pointing out that he might be lucky enough to elude the Raiders and to win through.

" If the Government will give me a military escort I will go, but not without," was his final word.

I had no authority to compel him to go on, so gave up the struggle. But I realised more than ever how imperative it was to endeavour to reach Robat without a moment's unnecessary delay, and start conclusions with the Raiders, whose menace was growing more dangerous every day.

We were, therefore, on the road very early next morning, for I hoped to make Saindak that night. I had intended to go by Borgar, but now that I knew—for I had verified the contractor's statements, and believed them to be correct—that that place was in the hands of the Raiders, I elected to go by an alternative route, known as the *Webb-Ware* route, which is practically out of use nowadays, hoping, thereby, to avoid the enemy.

It was still dark when we set off on the most strenuous part of our journey; climbing, making détours, digging the car out again and again till we were all three worn out in body and temper. We hardly halted that day, for the necessity for speed was as fully realised by Allan as by myself.

When night fell we had not yet sighted Saindak, but I knew we could not be very far off, and cursed the coming of the night which made it impossible to see where we were. I knew we had got off the camel track somehow, for the ground was even more bumpy than it had been, and was frequently intersected by nullahs or rocky ravines, which made the going positively dangerous. If the car were knocked right out of action our difficulties would reach the last stage of disaster.

At last, in despair, Allan stopped, saying it was useless going on any further. We might overturn the car at any moment and smash it as well as ourselves. He submitted that the only sane thing would be to camp just where we were and wait for daylight, when we might regain the camel track.

I knew he was right, but said I would make one final effort on foot to find the track, and directed him to give me the hurricane lamp we carried on the car.

Stumbling and slipping over the broken ground in the pitch darkness, the lamp barely lighting up my immediate path, I had wandered some distance from the car when I heard voices. Instantly I thought of the Raiders who were over-running the district. It would be too galling, too humiliating to be captured by them before the campaign, on which I was building such high hopes, had even begun.

Noiselessly I put out the lamp and listened in the dense darkness. There was absolute silence for some minutes, and I stood stock still. Then voices sounded again, and I conjectured that there were not more than two, or at the most three, speakers.

I thought rapidly, and finally decided that there would not be many men in front of me. Had there been anything approaching an encampment of the Raiders in the neighbourhood, there would have been lights, camp fires and considerable noise. The voices I had heard probably belonged to men who had seen the lights of the car, and had come to find out what it was.

I turned swiftly and made my way back to the car, where I had foolishly left my revolver. Recovering my weapon I warned Allan in a whisper of the voices I had heard, and told him to be ready to stand by. Then I made my way back in the darkness, and when I had regained the spot, called out loudly, in Hindustani, " Who's there? "

Instantly a voice answered, " I am Idu of the Chagai Levies, friendly to the British Government."

I then called out who I was, and, immediately, three fully armed men came forward in the darkness.

I asked them what they were doing there, and the voice that had answered me before replied that they were all three members of the Chagai Levies, and that they, and about fifty others, had come out to fight me.

"To fight me?" I exclaimed. "Whatever for?"

"Well, Sahib," returned the man who had said his name was Idu, "we thought you were a German airship." And he went on to explain that for a long time he and his companions had been watching powerful lights floating about in the sky, and as they knew that Germans were the only people in the world who had *hawaiijihaz* or airships, they were convinced the lights they had seen belonged to one of these. And when it had alighted on the hill in front of them, the majority of his companions had been so terrified that they had run away, and only himself and his two comrades had had the bravery to stay where they were and face the unknown danger.

Then it dawned on me what he was driving at. The flashing electric lights of the car, lighting up the distant, rising slopes of the desert, had appeared to these men to come from the sky, and my harmless motor-car the dreaded German airship. Cars, of course, along this route were as great a novelty as airships, and doubtless not one of the men in front of me had ever seen one before.

I reassured them as completely as I could, adding that I was delighted to meet such redoubtable warriors, and hoped that now they would come with me and help me, as my business was to fight Germans, airships and all. This was strictly true, for, but for German influence, there would have been no need to wage war on the Raiders who had only been induced to become our enemies by lying German propaganda.

Idu said they would be only too glad to go with the Sahib and to help him fight the enemies of the British Raj. He also told me that he had already saved my life once that evening.

"How was that?" I asked, my spirits rising as I gazed through the darkness at my first three recruits.

"Well, Sahib," returned Idu, "when the airship, which you say is no airship, stopped, in a little while we saw the figure of a man, carrying a lantern moving towards us, and Halil here," laying his hand on the shoulder of one of his pals, "lifted his rifle and was about to shoot. But I said, 'Nay. See, it is but one man. Let us wait and see who he is.' And then the lantern went out and there was no longer a target."

"You did well, Idu," I said solemnly. "You have most certainly saved my life, and as you seem to be as intelligent as you are brave, I shall appoint you to my personal staff. I am the officer who has been sent out to take command of the forces along the Sarhad, and in Seistan. But at the present moment my chief concern is to find the right road to Saindak. Can you show it to me?"

Idu laughed. "I could lead you there blindfold, Sahib."

I felt the difficulties of the road were now over, and, piloted by these three stalwarts, the car—a source of the utmost excitement and wonderment to them—Allan, Allah-dad and my weary self were, ere long, safe in the rest-house of the small mud fort at Saindak.

The following morning, after a good night's rest, I had a long talk with Idu, and the very favourable impression I had formed of the man the night before was greatly increased. I found him by daylight to be a highly intelligent-looking, splendidly proportioned fellow of about five feet eight, with a big black beard. I had glimpses, even then, of the keen sense of humour which was to do so much to lighten the difficulties of the ensuing campaign. Never once in all the months to come did I find his wit and humour fail.

As after-events proved he was absolutely invaluable. In fact, I often called him, and told him that I called him, my "head." Not only did he know every yard of the country, but he knew by name practically every one of the Raiders, knew their peculiarities and their weak points as well as their strength. Idu was a man in a million, and I should like to think that, some day, this public appreciation of him, and of what he did to help in this campaign, may reach him.

After breakfast and my talk with Idu, we set out on the last march of the first phase of my journey, and reached Robat by two o'clock in the afternoon.

CHAPTER III

A PLAN OF CAMPAIGN

An "intelligent" officer—Matters political—Three tribes and a fourth—Their women and inter-tribal laws—Sarhad conditions—A summons to the Chiefs—A bid for rank—Telegraph wires and Sheitan—Two first-class liars—A strategic scheme—An ungazetted General—Lost kit—Swallows and flies—Forces available—Communications freed—The Kacha levy and a shock—Mirjawa.

My first visit in Robat was to the officer who had been commanding the scattered British forces up to that date. He was a very sick man, and had been holding out with the utmost difficulty until he could be relieved. Here I met Major Landon of the 35th Scinde Horse, one of the three Intelligence Officers employed by the Indian Government in Persia.

I very quickly realised that Landon was an officer of very high intelligence, as well as an Intelligence Officer, and that he had a fund of information concerning the country, and the conditions and characteristics of the inhabitants of both Persia and Baluchistan. In fact, I judged that he would be such an asset that, then and there, I invited him to become my Brigade-Major, although I ruefully remarked that I had, at present, no brigade!

He was keen to accept, but did not know how the authorities at Simla would view his acceptance of such a post, and asked me whether I should be willing to shoulder the responsibility of annexing him for the campaign. Considering that my shoulders were broad enough, I promptly replied that my orders had been to take command of all the scattered forces I could find and co-ordinate them, and that I looked upon him as my second "find," Idu and his two companions being the first. Further, that he was here as Intelligence Officer and would acquire no intelligence sitting down in Robat, whereas, if he came with me, he would get all he wanted at first hand!

I set myself to pick up all the information I could about the conditions of British "influence" in this part of Persia, and on the borders of Afghanistan. To make it in any way clear why we had any influence here at all we must revert to the old fear of the threatened advance of Russia on India, in the days before Russia became our ally in the Great War.

Slowly and gradually Russia had been extending her influence in the Pamirs until her outposts on the Oxus River were only eight marches from Chitral. Evidently, as a wide counter, strategic move, the Indian Government had sought to increase its own influence with Persia and Afghanistan by pushing forward her outposts to Robat and Nasaratabad.

Consequently, at the time of which I am writing, Robat, Nasaratabad and Birjand were held lightly by chains of small posts composed entirely of Indian troops and some local levies commanded by British officers. Our lines of communication running from Birjand to Nushki, a distance of about six hundred miles, were held, in widely scattered posts, by only one battalion of Indian Infantry and one regiment of Indian Cavalry and four mountain guns. Thus it will be seen that it was very difficult to obtain any troops for a movable column.

A British Consulate had also been established at Nasaratabad, which is on the borders of Afghanistan and Persia. During the War the importance and influence of the Consul increased considerably, as he was in a position to gather information which was of great value to the military commanders, who constantly sought his advice.

There was also a Baluch Political Officer, known as the Sarhad-dar, who worked under orders from the British Political Officer at Quetta. The Sarhad-dar, to a certain degree, controlled the Sarhadi Raiders, occasionally with the help of the Chagai Levies, which were raised by the Indian Government for this particular work.

Supplies were brought to these scattered posts by camel caravans from India.

Communication with India was maintained by means of the telegraph. Later on it became necessary to send out a wireless troop from India to establish communication between my force at Khwash and Saindak.

At the same time I did my best to learn all I could about the tribes amongst whom I was going to operate, their ways and customs, and the nature of the country in which they lived.

A glance at the map will show the situation and boundaries of the Sarhad—literally meaning boundary. It will be seen that it extends from Jalk in the East to Galugan in the West. The Eastern part, from Jalk to Safed-koh, is held by a tribe known as the Gamshadzais, under their notable leader, Halil Khan.

The central portion is held by the Yarmahommedzais under Jiand Khan, an elderly man, who has been undisputed chief, and a sort of over-lord of the whole of the Sarhad, for very many years. He has been looked upon by his own and neighbouring tribes as well-nigh a demi-god. As Jiand enters later, and largely, into this narrative all further description of him will be reserved till actual contact is established with him.

Khwash—known also as Vasht or Washt—is the capital of the Sarhad, and is situated within Jiand's jurisdiction, although he is not the actual owner of the town. The word Khwash literally means "sweet," and, I believe, owes its name to the water, which is, by the way, quite warm when it appears at the surface of the ground in the immediate vicinity.

The Western portion of the Sarhad, extending roughly from Khwash to Galugan, is held by the Ismailzais under their redoubtable leader, Juma Khan.

All three of these tribes possess approximately

one thousand families apiece, and, of course, each family has many members, as well as large numbers of camels, and herds of sheep and goats.

Each of these tribes, at the time of which I write, could muster, roughly, from one to two thousand riflemen, chiefly armed with Mauser rifles and modern ammunition.

South of Robat lay a fourth tribe, the Rekis, fewer in number than any one of those already mentioned. This tribe was entirely friendly to the British, and, although nominally under a leader called Ibrahim, paid more heed to Idu, who, as I have already said, was one of the most remarkable men I have ever had the pleasure of meeting. He was also a Havildar (Sergeant) in the Chagai Levies; a local force raised by the Indian Government.

These various tribes all belong to the Sunni branch of the Mahommedan religion, and are of Arab origin. As a whole they are a fine-looking set of men, slim and graceful, with fine, intelligent faces, and aquiline features. Their hair is allowed to grow unrestricted, and falls in long black ringlets, on either side of the face, in true King Charles I. style. In fact, one of these men, with whom I afterwards made good friends, was nicknamed Charles I. on sight, as, with his flowing ringlets and short pointed beard, he bore such a strong resemblance to the pictures of that unfortunate monarch.

These men are fine skirmishers, and will fight with the utmost bravery when well led, and have confidence in their leaders. Being nomads, they possess but few villages, such as Khwash, Gusht, and Jalk; which consist of a mud fort or forts and a few houses. Their lives are spent for the most part in tents, called Jugis, which are made of camels' hair, dyed black, and are pitched wherever a convenient spot can be found.

Wives, families and herds accompany them on their wanderings from place to place. Their womenkind are often good-looking, and usually lighter skinned than the men. The women's endurance, too, is wonderful, for they can climb the precipitous hills with as much agility as the men, bear the hardships of long marches, the violent summer heat and the intense cold of the winter nights with great fortitude. They go unveiled, and appear to be treated well by their husbands and sons. In fact, in some notable instances, the women of the Sarhad exercise great influence over their husbands, and, when this is so, rule with the proverbial "rod of iron." Each man is allowed four wives, and, though he does not always acquire this number, he never exceeds it.

The tribes literally live by raiding. They know no fear, and seldom show mercy. They not only raid travellers but villages, and, on occasion, large towns. These raids have been known to be pushed as far as Meshed, the sacred town and "Mecca" of Persia, which lies far away in the North upon the Turkestan border. Such expeditions are carried out with immense skill and cunning, and are seldom unsuccessful. The raiders not only loot jewels, carpets, food, cattle and herds, but women and children, whom they subject to a life of utter misery.

Persian ladies are frequently carried off in this way, to become eventually abject slaves subject to inter-tribal barter. The prices paid for such slaves naturally vary according to quality, age and looks. As much as three hundred rupees may be taken as an average price for a young woman, and as little as twenty-five rupees for a small child.

But, although they are utterly lawless in regard to other people, their few inter-tribal laws are fairly strictly observed. These laws, however, chiefly consist of the doctrine that Might is Right and Success pardons all Sins. In the Sarhad a man is expected to tell the truth—unless a lie better suits his purpose. Any oath given on the Koran is binding, provided a Mullah or priest is present. Otherwise such an oath is as often honoured in the breach as in the observance.

They have, however, some standards of honour to which they strictly adhere. If, for instance, they come as invited guests to your camp, or if you go as an invited guest to theirs, treachery is not thought of. The laws of hospitality, as in nearly all Eastern countries, are strictly maintained.

Their food consists mostly of flour-cake, made, as a rule, of barley, though occasionally of wheat, and goat-flesh and wild herbs. As their herds always travel with them, except when fighting or raiding, there is always a plentiful supply of meat and milk. Their slaves, on the contrary, are half starved, and present the most pitiful contrast to their own women and children, who are well fed, healthy and provided with ample clothing.

Their country, the Sarhad, is very arid, sandy, sparsely cultivated, and crossed by range upon range of bare volcanic hills, with rugged peaks and precipitous sides. Some of these hills rise to considerable heights, as, for example, the Koh-i-Bazman, overlooking Bampur in the South. This peak reaches an altitude of eleven thousand four hundred feet. The Koh-i-Taftan is another, of something over thirteen thousand feet, and is snow-capped in Winter and early Spring, despite the fact that it is an active volcano. The word Taftan signifies boiling. Its crater possesses two main outlets, from which clouds of sulphur-smoke are constantly being emitted. The whole summit is in consequence covered with white ash, so giving it a wonderfully imposing and picturesque appearance from a distance, especially at sunset or sunrise. The effect is very like that of Fuji-Yama, but certainly on a grander scale.

The hills of this district are all of volcanic origin, and, for this reason, rich in sulphur and sal-ammoniac deposits. The low-lying country obviously once formed the bed of a sea, for the fossils to be found here in quantity are of marine origin, and the soil is thickly impregnated with salt. Fresh water is very scarce, though large salt water lakes are fairly frequent.

It is interesting to think how much could be done with this country were some scheme of irrigation introduced. The natives have a simple method of supplying water to meet their wants. This is done by means of karezes, underground channels which tap underground springs and so bring the water to where it is wanted.

Trees are occasionally planted by these karezes, in the towns, but otherwise are scarcely ever seen in this inhospitable, arid region, where it is even hard to find sufficient food for camels, horses or herds, when on the march. There are occasional valleys through which a small stream may flow for a certain distance, but which, very soon, disappears again into the sand. In those rare spots where water is plentiful the luxuriance of the vegetation is phenomenal, proving how fertile the country might become were it irrigated in the same way as are certain parts of India. Wheat, barley, spinach, cucumbers, pumpkins and green vegetables grow readily where water exists.

Climatic conditions in these regions are curiously extreme. Great cold prevails in the Winter, but the heat in Spring and Summer is terrific. There is, too, a curious feeling of intense lightness in the atmosphere which induces a queer feeling of "emptiness" in those unaccustomed to its rarified quality. A hot wind, impregnated with sand, blows in Seistan more or less continually from April to July, so adding to the general discomfort of the white man. This wind is known as the Sad-o-bistroz (literally, " wind which blows for one hundred and twenty days "). But, though disagreeable and irritating, this wind saves the health of the Seistani inhabitants during the most trying months of the year, as it checks malaria by blowing away the mosquitoes.

This rather vague, and very incomplete, attempt at a sketch of the people who were causing such serious trouble to our Government, and of the country in which they lived, may, at any rate, serve to give some idea of the foe, and his terrain, in this small but terse campaign which I shall make an attempt to describe in the following chapters.

It grew more evident daily that it was necessary to organise a movable column to operate against the Raiders as soon as possible.

There were more troops at Nasaratabad than at any other post, and I considered that some of these might well be taken for the purpose. Moreover, there was a British Consul there whose advice and information would be very valuable. Accordingly, Landon and I arranged to go there by car on the first possible day.

But I thought it would be a good preliminary move to find out exactly how the land lay with regard to the Raiders, and to force them, so to speak, to declare their policy towards us.

I therefore told the local Baluchi political officer to send out notices to Jiand Khan, the leader of the Yarmahommedzais, to Halil Khan, the leader of the Gamshadzais, to Juma Khan, leader of the Ismailzais, and to the leader of the Rekis, to meet the new British General, just arrived from India, so that counsel might be taken together on a certain date at a small post called Kacha.

Of course, from all I had heard, I did not for one moment expect these Raider Chiefs to keep the *rendezvous*. But if, by some amazing chance, they did, we might come to some amicable arrangement and so avoid actual fighting. If, on the other hand, they refused to do so, it would be tantamount to a declaration of war.

A few days later I kept the appointment I had made, but, with the exception of the Reki leaders, who assured me of their consistent loyalty to the British, not a single Raider Chief turned up.

Thereupon I returned to Robat and planned my campaign.

Already I could see I was going to be badly handicapped by my lack of rank, and determined to make a bid for the rank which would give me more authority. With this object in view I sent a telegram to General Kirkpatrick—already mentioned as Chief of Staff at Simla, and acting as Commander-in-Chief in the absence of General Sir Beauchamp

Duff—asking him to make me a General, and stating baldly that I considered it necessary.

It may seem strange that, in this wild, desolate country, largely in the hands of lawless, rebellious tribes, it was possible to send a telegram at all. But a fine telegraph line, right across Persia, connecting Europe with India, has been in existence for over fifty years. The concession to erect this line was obtained from the Shah by Mr Eastwick in 1862, then British Chargé d'Affaires in Teheran.

There had been long negotiations over this concession, which had been consistently refused by the Persian Government; but the Shah's personal friendship for Mr Eastwick prevailed where diplomatic negotiations had failed. It was a particularly advantageous arrangement for us, as, by the contract drawn up by the Persian Government in 1864, that Government undertook to construct a telegraph line from the Persian frontier, near Baghdad, to India, at the expense of Persia, but to place it under the control of British officers. This and other telegraph lines had not been interfered with or cut in any way by the Raiders, for the simple reason that they have strong superstitious fears of telegraph wires, and imagine them in some way to be in close communication with Sheitans (devils).

Whilst I was awaiting a reply to my urgent request for an advance in rank, Idu, Landon and I took counsel together. I asked Idu whether he had two first-class liars amongst his friends, in whom he

" A GOOD LIAR."
Landon's orderly and chief spy.

could place implicit trust. His eyes twinkled as he assured me he had many friends on whose complete fidelity, as well as on whose absolute qualifications, he could rely.

I then unfolded to him my scheme. It was quite obvious that it would be utterly impossible to defeat the Raiders in open fight. They numbered several thousands of fully armed men, amply equipped, and supplied with all the ammunition and food they needed. They were also in their own country, every yard of which they knew well.

In a straightforward fight any small force we could muster would be wiped out in a few minutes. But as it was necessary to fight and beat those Raiders, who were doing us such immeasurable damage, bluff must be used to strengthen our arms.

I suggested to Idu that he should procure his two skilled friends and tell them, at the outset, that if they succeeded in the plan entrusted to them their pockets would be literally lined with rupees. They were, then, to run away from me to the two principal Raider Chiefs, Jiand and Halil Khan, and their story was to be that they had managed to escape from the great and famous British General who had just arrived with five thousand fully armed troops. Also, that this General Dyer was greatly incensed at their disobedient method of treating his summons to meet him at Kacha, and that he was starting in great force to attack them, but that he was planning to march first against Halil Khan in the direction of Jalk.

If Idu's men succeeded in making the Raiders swallow all this, the immediate stroke I had in view, namely, an attack on Khwash, might hope for some success. It would at any rate draw the Raiders off the lines of communication and so enable supply caravans to proceed to Robat.

Idu was greatly taken with the idea. It appealed to his sense of humour, and he had soon produced his two spies, on whom, he assured us, he could rely as on himself. Their mission fully explained, Idu's friends started off at once.

Meanwhile, though I was not yet a General I determined to act the part. The 28th Light Cavalry made crossed swords for my shoulders and the necessary red tabs. The former were considerably bigger than the regulation pattern, but were otherwise well made. Then Landon and I went off by car to Nasaratabad.

We found the place to be a small mud-walled enclosure with walls of great thickness. Inside the enclosure were something like a hundred shops, for the most part kept by Persian soldiers, whose military duties are not usually onerous. We made our way to the Consul's house, and had a very interesting interview with him. Whilst we were there a telegram arrived from Simla informing me that I had been promoted to the rank of Brigadier-General. This was a great relief, for I now no longer felt an impostor.

As a set-off against this bit of good news, I heard

that the whole of my kit, which had followed me from Nushki, had been captured by the Raiders. In addition they had killed my horse, Galahad, robbed the groom of all his clothing and torn his golden ear-rings from his ears. On my return to Robat he came to me stark naked, with his nerves utterly shattered, and absolutely useless for any further service.

We also met Colonel Claridge, who was commanding the 28th Cavalry and the troops at Nasaratabad. I asked him to send to Robat as soon as possible all the food supplies he could collect, two mountain guns, a squadron of cavalry, and as many infantry as he could spare. I was very disappointed, however, at the few troops available at Nasaratabad for the expedition, but I realised that the situation in Afghanistan demanded the presence of a fairly strong garrison at Nasaratabad itself.

On the way back to Robat we stopped at a post where I was accommodated in a room with a domed mud roof, which had been whitewashed. As I lay on my blankets in the morning, gazing up at the roof, I noticed that the dome was covered with small black spots. As the light grew stronger I realised that they were flies, thousands of them, in a comatose condition, owing to the cold of the night.

As the morning advanced, swallows flew in by the open door, and, fluttering round the dome, picked off the helpless flies one by one, until not a single one was left.

Directly we reached Robat Landon and I set to work on our plans. After considerable thought we determined to make an attempt to capture Khwash, the capital of the Sarhad, and so endeavour to entice the Raiders off our lines of communication. But it took some time to get the guns and food supplies to Robat, for Robat was quite one hundred miles from Nasaratabad. It was also necessary to get in enough supplies for a month at least, as it was useless placing reliance on anything reaching us from India. In other words we had to be quite independent of all lines of communication.

At last the two guns, and supplies, under Major MacGowan, reached Robat, where were now collected about a dozen or fifteen of Idu's Chagai Levies, and seventeen Sawars of the 28th Light Cavalry under Lieutenant Hirst. But I still had no infantry. That, however, I hoped to get at Kacha, the garrison of which consisted of a hundred sepoys of the 19th Punjab Infantry, and two maxim guns.

Therefore, Landon and I arranged to go to Kacha for the infantry, while MacGowan proceeded with his two guns, seventeen cavalrymen and supplies, direct to Mirjawa, via Saindak. We would then join him there, as soon as we had collected the infantry for our advance on Khwash.

Our real movements had been kept marvellously secret, whilst the news of the five thousand fully armed troops under my command had been spread far and near by Idu's spies; the consequence being that the Raiders were all quietly retiring, from raids upon our lines of communication, to organise their own *lashkars* (armies), and their own defence.

Thus, and at any rate temporarily, the lines of communication of our scattered frontier posts were cleared, and without striking a blow. One small objective had at least been accomplished.

While MacGowan's little force was making its way to Mirjawa, Landon and I rode to Kacha, reaching that place on the 2nd of April. There Lieutenant Yates, of the 12th Pioneers, paraded all the men he could lay his hands on in front of the mess-house, and, as we rode up, gave the order for the men to present arms.

The result was a shock.

I dismounted and called on all those men who had ever fired a shot in their lives to fall out.

To my dismay only nine men obeyed.

Lieutenant Yates told me that he had done his best with the men, but the greater proportion of them were mere raw recruits. It was a bitter disappointment, and it was very obvious that a great deal of brick-making had to be done without straw. But there was nothing else for it. These were the only men, trained or untrained, available for the expedition, and I had to be thankful for them.

I took the nine trained soldiers, sixty-five of the

untrained recruits, and two maxim guns belonging to the 12th Pioneers, and, with these, Landon and I made our way to the *rendezvous* at Mirjawa, where we all met on the evening of the 6th of April.

CHAPTER IV

BLUFF AND ARMS

Ladis and its fort—A force without arms—First sight of the enemy—Shah Sawar and more bluff—Battle—Bluff succeeds—Casualties—Bad news from the North—Idu's proposition—Jiand's stragglers—Jiand's white flag.

THE following day we marched to Ladis, reaching that place just before nightfall, and without incident.

Ladis is a camping place situated in a comparatively fertile tract of country fully four thousand feet above sea-level on the slopes of the famous Koh-i-taftan. A considerable stream flows through the valley. If this stream were exploited for irrigation purposes the whole district could be made most productive and profitable. The climate is far better than in the greater part of the Sarhad, and there is an abundance of chikor and other partridges, ibex, and wolves.

On the right bank of the stream is a fine old deserted fort, which is far more substantially built than the occupied forts of Khwash and Jalk, but it has been ruined by the disintegrating effect of the water on the banks on which it is built. A passage at the base of it indicates that at one time an underground tunnel connected the fort, which lies on the right bank, with the left bank, thus affording a means of escape, or of reinforcement, for the garrison.

We found, waiting for us at Ladis, a band of about fifty Rekis, who had come to join the expedition in answer to an urgent appeal from Idu.

I found they had no arms, ammunition or equipment, and asked them where their rifles were.

" We have none, Sahib," their spokesman replied. " We thought the General Sahib would give us rifles."

I was obliged to tell them that we had no spare arms, but as every extra man would be an asset in our great game of bluff I was not going to let them go, and would find some means of utilising their services.

At first they were greatly disappointed to find that they were not going to be awarded a free issue of British rifles, and commented on the absurdity of a force of the size they saw before them attempting to attack the great Raider Chief, Jiand Khan.

" Why, Sahib," the spokesman said, " Jiand has fully two thousand well-armed men, all out to meet you. They will wipe you out in about two minutes."

If it came to an open fight we all knew that this was literally true. But we were relying on bluff and luck.

The local political officer, a Baluch, was entirely of the Rekis' way of thinking, and did his utmost to persuade us to turn back and save our skins. But we had not come so far to turn back. Orders were, therefore, given to go forward.

Fortunately for us, and before we struck camp early on the following morning, another political officer arrived to supersede him—a man of totally different calibre. Khan-Bahadur, the Sarhad-dar (the chief political officer of all matters concerning the Sarhad) was full of fight, greatly taken with our game of bluff, and fully prepared to enter into its spirit, the only spirit which could possibly bring such an enterprise as ours to a successful conclusion.

From Ladis the force marched South in the direction of Khwash, covering about eighteen miles. This was not bad going when it is remembered that the average rate for a camel caravan over rough sandy country of this sort is about ten or twelve miles a day. We camped that night in a narrow valley, surrounded by hills, and with a good water supply.

The following day the march was resumed, and we were beginning to wonder how soon we should get in touch with Jiand's forces when our advance scouts reported that the enemy was just ahead, and encamped on the low hills running out in spurs from the Koh-i-Taftan.

Our force was halted, and, riding forward myself, I dismounted and took a good look at the enemy's position. This appeared to be, as I had to admit to myself, a very strong one, and, as far as I could gather, it looked as if it had been no idle report that

Jiand's force numbered something like two thousand men. In any case we were in for it now, and must take our chances as they came.

I rode back, ordered the mountain guns to be brought up to some low hills on the left, and the cavalry to move forward under cover to the right.

The transport camels, numbering about six hundred, now came up, under cover, and were put in charge of the sixty-five untrained infantrymen. The two machine guns were brought up to a favourable position in the centre, and our little force was now fully deployed for action.

At this moment a man mounted on a camel was seen coming from the enemy's camp, accompanied by a man on foot carrying a white flag of truce.

When the messenger had approached nearer the Sarhad-dar exclaimed, "Why, it is Shah Sawar himself!"

Now Shah Sawar was a very famous Raider Chief, and a relation of Jiand's. At one time he had been the owner and governor of Khwash, but it appears that he had greatly coveted, as a bride, a very beautiful lady known as the Gul-Bibi, or Rose Lady. As usual, negotiations were conducted between the prospective bridegroom and the lady's nearest male relative, who, in this instance, happened to be a somewhat weak-charactered man named Mahommed-Hassan. The price that Mahommed-Hassan placed on the Gul-Bibi was no less than the ownership of Khwash itself. Shaw Sawar's infatu-

QUESTIONING A SARHADI PRISONER.

ation drove him to pay the price, though, from what I came to know of the ruffian afterwards, I am perfectly convinced that he had every intention of recovering his patrimony as soon as a favourable opportunity presented itself.

When he rode up to me, preceded by the flag of truce, I was struck by his fine appearance.

He announced that he had come with a message from his kinsman, Jiand Khan, to the effect that, "If the General Sahib, accompanied by only one man, would meet Jiand half-way, Jiand, also accompanied by one man, would meet him and discuss the situation."

Of course the very last thing I wanted to do was to prolong any negotiations. Every moment that passed increased the danger that our bluff would be discovered, for it was quite obvious that, up to date, Jiand believed in the existence of the great force being brought against him under a British General, as reported to him by Idu's spies. Therefore, it was necessary to bluster, and answer indignantly, "How dare you come to a British General with any such proposal from a scoundrel like Jiand? Go back and tell him that I am coming, not half-way, but the whole way, and at once. I will give you time to take him my message. I will then fire a shot into the air as the signal that hostilities have begun, and the attack, which will wipe him out, will commence."

Shah Sawar was visibly impressed, and, after a

few moments' hesitation, beckoned to the man who had come with him. After a whispered colloquy the latter returned to Jiand with the General Sahib's message. Shah Sawar himself said that he intended to remain with me.

He was obviously cowed and bewildered. He firmly believed we had a great army in the low hills behind us, and deemed it safer to remain with us as a prisoner than to return to Jiand's camp and engage in a battle against five thousand troops—which he could not see from his present position!

Whilst the messenger was racing back to Jiand the seventeen cavalrymen were ordered to show themselves, and as they topped the hills, apparently the advance guard of a great force, their big horses looked most imposing.

Lieutenant Hirst, commanding them, was directed to make a pretence of threatening the left flank and rear of Jiand's position, but ordered not to go too close!

Then, as soon as information came that Jiand's messenger had reached his camp—some six hundred yards distant—and had had time to deliver his message, one of the Chagai Levies was ordered to fire a shot into the air as a signal that the battle had begun.

He pulled his trigger, but nothing happened.

I told him to try again.

Again he pulled the trigger, and this time with the desired result.

The battle had begun.

The order to charge was given. The cavalry moved rapidly to the right, the machine guns rattled, and the infantry—nine trained men and a handful of Chagai Levies, rushed forward in the centre.

What happened in the enemy's camp I only learned afterwards, but it appears to have been as follows: Jiand, seeing the cavalry advancing as if to threaten his retreat, really believed that the mythical army of five thousand was commencing its attack in full force, and, mounting his own camel, he gave an order which literally amounted to a "*sauve qui peut*." In any case, and in a moment, his force was scattered in a frenzy of terror, and in full retreat, amongst the hills and valleys.

For a moment Landon and I looked at each other. Then, as we realised that the great bluff had succeeded, we rushed forward, with a loud whoop, closely accompanied by the Sarhad-dar. As we were mounted, we got ahead of the others, and actually overtook a number of Jiand's men retreating down a nullah. We emptied our revolvers into them, and some of our infantry coming up, their terror was increased, for they thought they had been trapped by overwhelming numbers.

The enemy had suffered a loss of seven killed. On our side we had one man wounded, and I honestly believe he was wounded by one of our own untrained infantrymen, who, in the excitement and enthusiasm of the moment, had disobeyed orders and joined in the chase.

By the evening there was no one left in sight to chase, so we halted and made preparations to camp where we were. Only a few hours before we had known that if the truth of our numbers had leaked out not one of us would live till night to tell the tale. Fortunately the secret had been well kept, and, although we had only accounted for seven of the enemy, it was obvious we had won a decisive victory. Jiand's entire force was scattered and demoralised, and it would take him a considerable time, even when he did learn how he had been tricked, to collect them again.

He was a very notable man, with enormous power and prestige, not only with his own tribe, the Yarmahommedzais, but with all the nomad tribes of the district, and was regarded as a personage by the Governments of both India and of Persia. His defeat would be a very bitter pill for him to swallow. Although he was looked on by the Ismailzais and the Gamshadzais as a sort of over-lord, even of their own Chiefs, there was always great rivalry between the various tribes, and he would know that Juma Khan, whilst outwardly sympathising with him, would, in reality, be jubilant.

Accordingly, and for the sake of his own prestige, he must make the most of the forces brought against him. That very evening I learned from one of his men, who had been overtaken and brought back as a prisoner, that he had given out that he had had seven hundred men killed and amongst the number was his own favourite son. The death of this son, I afterwards found, was a bitter blow to the famous old Chief, and I have always been sorry that he credited my hand as being the one which had struck him down, though this was absolutely untrue.

Seven men multiplied by a hundred was not bad as a free advertisement. But I determined to go one better.

"Seven hundred!" I retorted to the trembling prisoner. "Nonsense! If you had said seven thousand, it would be far nearer the mark."

Now the great thing was to make the most of our almost bloodless victory near Koh-i-taftan, and pursue Jiand and his men as far as possible amongst the rocky fastnesses of the hills into which they had fled. If only the old ruffian could be persuaded to surrender before the bluff was called, it would be just possible to make the other tribes think that the whole game was up, and so make terms with us; thus obviating a long and harassing campaign.

So we pursued him for two days, as far as Kamalabad, his own special winter headquarters, nearly overtaking him. But he just eluded us as we entered the place by riding out at the other end, and so escaped into the Morpeish Hills, where it was quite hopeless to think of following him with our very small force.

On the other hand, if we left him there, he became an hourly menace. It could be only a question of time before Jiand would be bound to learn how he had been duped. He would then collect his men once more, summon the other tribes to his assistance, and wipe out our little force as he might have done, had he only known, at Koh-i-taftan.

Moreover, news had just reached us of an untoward little incident which had occurred away to the West of Robat. A small British force had been operating in the vicinity of Nasaratabad-sippi (not to be confused with Nasaratabad in Seistan) and this force had been attacked in overwhelming numbers by the Ismailzais, under Juma Khan. It had suffered considerable loss, not only in men, but in mules, rifles, and, most important of all, ammunition. The British officer commanding had fought ably and had averted disaster, but the losses had been sufficient to create a rumour that Juma Khan had scored an exaggerated victory.

This must undoubtedly be avenged, and the only hope of doing so was to strike at once, and whilst Jiand's forces were still scattered and demoralised.

Landon, the Sarhad-dar, Idu and I immediately took counsel together. We discussed the reports of the various scouts who had been sent out in every direction. It appeared that the redoubtable Jiand had received a great shock, and that his nerves were thoroughly shattered. He had dearly loved his son, and the loss was a great grief. He also firmly believed he had lost a great number of his followers in killed and wounded, and his pride was suffering badly in the loss of his prestige as a practically unbeaten Chief.

Then Idu evolved a brilliant scheme by which he believed we should be able to lure Jiand, in his present broken state, to surrender. Kamalabad, where we were at present encamped, and which was Jiand's favourite winter residence, is one of the few spots in the Sarhad well irrigated and consequently well cultivated. The place is freely intersected with karezes, from which the fields are systematically watered. Moreover, the valley is watered on its Western side by a stream which gushes out of the ground, and, after flowing past Gazo, winds round the Northern slopes of the Morpeish Hills and the Sar-i-drokan, to lose itself soon afterwards in the sand.

Kamalabad is not, strictly speaking, a village, as there are no houses there. But it becomes densely populated when Jiand's nomad families camp there in their *jugis* during the winter months.

Beyond this fertile valley, which for half the year is teeming with life, though it is practically deserted during the summer months, the Morpeish Hills rise abruptly and precipitately out of the plain to a height of ten thousand feet.

On the farther side of these hills, and shut in beyond by the Sar-i-drokan Range, rising to about the same height as the Morpeish Hills, and running parallel with them for a distance of about seventy-five miles, is another valley, Jiand's favourite summer haunt.

It will thus be seen that it was utterly impossible to think of attempting to drive Jiand out of his refuge. Even supposing that we succeeded in dislodging him from the Morpeish Hills he would at once make for the Sar-i-drokan, a range which would be still more difficult to negotiate, apart from the fact that it would draw us farther and farther from our base and any hope of supplies. But it was evident that something must be done, and done quickly. Idu's proposal was, therefore, the only one offering any hope of success.

All the crops of wheat and barley in the Kamalabad Valley were then at their full growth, though still green, and it was upon these crops, when harvested, that Jiand and the entire Yarmahommedzai tribe relied for their yearly bread supply.

Idu's idea was substantially this, that we should send a message to Jiand, whilst he still believed himself pursued by a vast force, summon him to surrender forthwith, and tell him that, if he failed to comply with the instant summons, the whole of his crops would be destroyed. Anyhow the idea was worth trying.

Accordingly, trustworthy messengers were sent to him telling him that if he surrendered himself on behalf of his tribe, before sundown on the following day, the lives of himself and his followers would be safe, and his crops would be spared. If, however, he failed to surrender by the appointed time, six hundred camels, which had already arrived with the advance guard of the great force operating against him, would be turned loose in his fields, and, as he well knew, would make very short work of his crops.

The hours that passed between the sending out of the messengers, and the time limit for Jiand's surrender, were very anxious ones. Would bluff continue to carry us through, or had the bubble been pricked?

During that day news reached us from stragglers, who came trembling to join us at Kamalabad, that many of the old people and women of Jiand's tribe were in great distress. During the headlong flight of himself and his fighting men the weaklings were left behind, and, in their terror, they had fled into all sorts of hiding places where there was neither water nor food. Orders were immediately given that they were to be reassured and succoured in every way, and that food and water were to be supplied to them, also *jugis*, wherever possible, to shelter them.

The day passed and the time limit was rapidly running out when, between four and five o'clock in the afternoon, we saw a little group of men emerge from the Morpeish Hills, carrying a white flag.

These men approached and announced that they had come as emissaries from Jiand Khan, who was on his way to surrender. He admitted his defeat by the overwhelming numbers brought against him, said he knew it was no use continuing to fight against them, and that his heart was broken by the loss of his son. For the sake of his people he must save the crops or they would surely die. Therefore, if the General Sahib swore on his honour that the lives of himself and his men would be safe, and that his crops would be spared, he would surrender.

CHAPTER V

KHWASH AND MORE BLUFF

Jiand's surrender—A political lecture—Jiand's oath—Bluff for Khwash—The army moves forward—Khwash and its fort—Mahommed-Hassan comes in—Beetles as scavengers—Halil Khan comes in—Rifle prices, a comparison—Idu's warning—News of Izzat—Order of march—Bluff for Bampur—The meteor hole.

At five o'clock Jiand arrived riding a camel, and followed by a few attendants.

I went forward to meet him, and treated him with all the courtesy due to his position.

He dismounted and offered his salaams. He was a fine but pathetic-looking figure—a tall, spare man—but the weight of years, and the strain of recent events, were beginning to bow his shoulders. His thick beard was quite grey, but his eyes could still flash with passion and anger, though, at present, they were dulled with grief and humiliation.

I immediately offered him my condolences on the death of his son, and told him I had heard that he believed that I personally was responsible for his death. I assured him that this was not so, and that I greatly regretted that so valiant a father should suffer the loss of a valiant son. I then invited him to sit down on a small rise of ground where a few sparse bushes offered some shade from the sun, and as we had no seats we sat down on the ground round him.

I pointed out to Jiand his folly in having proved false to the traditional friendship which had existed between him, his tribes and the British Raj. I also told him that I knew perfectly well he had been misled by German lies as to the breaking of British power, coupled with advice to harry the British lines of communication, and to help himself to all supplies upon which he could lay his hands before the German forces advanced into India, for, when they did, nothing much would be left to take. But, I asked him, how could a man of his intelligence have ever allowed himself to be gulled in such a manner? Had he thought, he must have known that British might was far too firmly established to be overthrown by anything so despicable as the German race, and he must have known too that, in deserting his old friends the British, and in fighting against them, he was only courting disaster.

I further asked him if he had ever, with his own eyes, seen one of the German airships which they had been boasting were flying everywhere, destroying enemy's lands, towns and herds. Jiand admitted that he had not.

I asked him how it came about that, if he had

JIAND'S MEN COMING IN TO PARLEY

really believed so much in the strength and power of the Germans, not one of them was to be found in the district to come to his help in his present difficulties? Either they were cowards and had run away, or they had lied to him and there had never been any German forces sweeping on victoriously to wipe out the British Raj.

Jiand admitted the force of all my arguments, and replied that he, and all the Sarhadis, had been grossly deceived, but pleaded that he himself had done his best to restrain his men from interfering with the British lines of communication, warning them that it was neither safe nor wise. However, he could not seriously have expected that I would swallow this excuse, as he was known to be held in such awe by his followers that not one of them would have dared to dispute his authority.

I demanded the return of all government camels and stores and of my kit, captured between Nushki and Robat, and he assured me that everything should be sent back in full.

While we were talking I noticed his eyes kept wandering round, and, at last, he could restrain his curiosity no longer, and asked me point blank where the vast mass of troops was which had conquered his own.

I replied, "It was not necessary to bring all my men to Kamalabad. I only came here with my advance guard to make you my prisoner. We have yet to capture Khwash."

The rest was left to his imagination.

His parole was then demanded, which he promptly gave, and solemnly swore, on the Koran, that neither he nor any of his tribe, would raise a hand again against the British Raj.

Neither he nor the handful of men he had brought with him, were disarmed. We had to continue our game of bluff and had to show that we were not in the least afraid of him.

After I had dismissed him, telling him he would accompany me wherever I went under open arrest, Landon, the Sarhad-dar, Idu and myself took counsel together as to the best way to obtain the surrender of Khwash with its fort, the main stronghold of the Yarmahommedzais.

We decided to send a couple of Landon's scouts direct to Khwash—about nineteen miles distant—with a message to Mahommed-Hassan, telling him that Jiand was a prisoner in my hands, and that he himself admitted a loss of seven hundred men killed in open fight with my forces, but that the figure was an under-estimate. Shah Sawar was also a prisoner in my hands. I called on him, therefore, to surrender the fort of Khwash to me before twelve, noon, on the following day, or warned him I should blow the whole place to the skies. Nor should I hold myself responsible for the future action of my troops.

Idu's eyes twinkled. "Just suppose, General Sahib, that Mahommed-Hassan refuses; may I ask how you propose to blow Khwash to the skies—or anywhere?"

I replied with becoming dignity that I should of course blow it to the skies with my artillery.

Idu roared with laughter. He said he had seen my pop-guns firing and he was afraid that, unless our bluff could do the trick, I should be unpleasantly surprised at the strength of the walls of Khwash.

The next morning our entire force of two mountain guns, two machine guns, seventeen cavalrymen, nine trained and sixty-five untrained infantry and a handful of Chagai Levies, moved forward to the assault of the Raiders' stronghold. By eleven o'clock, and while we were still about three miles distant, we came into full view of the fort. Even from that distance I could see that Idu's boast as to its strength was no idle one, and that if Mahommed-Hassan elected to put up a fight we could not possibly expect to be able to take it by assault.

Our anxieties were now further increased by rumours that Halil Khan, with all his Gamshadzais, was on the way to reinforce Jiand, of whose personal surrender he had not yet heard.

Our objective, Khwash, lay on a plateau about six miles wide, bordered on either side by two ranges of hills. These hills have an altitude of some six thousand feet and run parallel to each other on the North-East and South-West sides of the fort. The fort itself is somewhere about four thousand five hundred feet above sea-level. This plateau was at one time well populated, well wooded and cultivated with some seventy-three karezes running along it, all tapping the great underground stream which flows from the Southern slopes of the Koh-i-taftan.

We were hot and played out after our sixteen-mile march, so halted to rest, and to speculate as to whether Mahommed-Hassan would surrender on, or before, the time-limit given him.

We had not long to wait, however, for hardly had we halted when we saw a messenger, on foot and carrying a white flag, coming towards us.

He salaamed as he reached us and said he bore a message from Mahommed-Hassan, imploring me not to blow Khwash into the skies, as he had heard all about the defeat of the Yarmahommedzais under Jiand, and that, under the circumstances, he recognised the folly of attempting to oppose my advance. Moreover, he was now on his way to surrender himself and the fort.

So bluff still held the day!

And sure enough, a few minutes later, Mahommed-Hassan, a miserable-looking creature, arrived and tendered his formal surrender.

As we marched forward in style to enter the fort the Yarmahommedzai garrison marched out and joined the local population of "Khwashis," who have lived in and around the fort for many generations. These latter are peaceful cultivators

KHWASH FORT.

of the soil, and are allowed to exist because they are useful servants to Jiand and his fighting men.

They and their womenfolk are graciously allowed to keep a certain proportion of the crops they grow, the bulk of which goes to Jiand. These Khwashis are a much lower type of humanity than the Raiders, and only ask to be allowed to exist in peace.

The fort, on closer inspection, proved to be some seventy yards square, with two gates, one to the South-East and one to the North-West. The outer walls rise to about thirty feet with towers at the four corners, three of which are about thirty-five feet high, while the fourth is probably fully fifty feet. This latter tower was the one occupied by the garrison.

Of the seventy-three fine karezes originally existing in and around the fort we could only find two. But one of these was a particularly good one whose waters came to the surface and flowed outside the South-East walls in an extraordinarily clear and limpid stream, in refreshing contrast to so many of the tepid, brackish streams found throughout the Sarhad.

But the one feature of the neighbourhood which struck me most forcibly was the quantity of beetles to be found everywhere. Never in my life have I seen so many. They were of the variety commonly known as dung-beetles. This kind is larger than the ordinary house beetle, round and flat, jet black, and can fly, which adds to its unpleasantness. Directly occasion offers it flies from every direction and is soon rapidly and effectively at work. As a scavenger, unpleasant as it is, it undoubtedly represents a provision of nature to keep the place—where sanitation is unknown—clean and healthy.

A few trees are scattered round Khwash, and a welcome sight these were after unending vistas of sandy waste and bare hillside.

The country in the close vicinity of Khwash was well cultivated, whilst I noted with satisfaction that some of the hill slopes were covered with a tall grass. This would prove invaluable as fodder for the horses.

That same day another piece of good news reached us, to the effect that Halil Khan, the great leader of the Gamshadzais, had just heard of the surrender of Jiand, also the full details of his great defeat, and loss of seven hundred men. But beyond this the news ran that he was coming himself to surrender, and to tell me that he had seen the folly of his past actions.

Upon receipt of this news Landon and I looked at each other and then roared with laughter. We began to realise that the Battle of Koh-i-taftan had indeed been a decisive victory!

That same evening Halil Khan, and about fifty of his chosen men, arrived, and, formally salaaming, surrendered themselves. I was immensely impressed by the appearance of this Raider Chief.

He was not very tall, but was magnificently proportioned and developed, with an intelligent, handsome head, and a peculiarly alert look. He certainly looked what he was well known to be, namely, one of the best fighting leaders in the Sarhad.

He and all his men were armed with Mauser rifles and an abundance of ammunition. Halil Khan seemed wedded to his, and when he was informed that the General Sahib was going to extend to him the same terms as to Jiand and allow him to keep his rifle, his joy was very apparent.

These German rifles had either been provided by the Germans, and sent direct across Persia, or were the outcome of the gun-running in the Persian Gulf prior to the War.

The price of a Mauser in the Sarhad, at that time, was about one thousand one hundred rupees, though I was glad to learn that the British Lee-Enfield was valued at one thousand two hundred rupees. The real cost of manufacturing these rifles is, I believe, from six to ten pounds or sixty to one hundred rupees, so that it will be seen what sort of a price the Raiders are prepared to pay for their arms.

Halil Khan was particularly anxious to learn how we had managed to defeat Jiand, and was of course curious to know where the vast British forces were. But he gathered no more information than Jiand had done.

My own private opinion is that Halil Khan was

disgusted with Jiand for surrendering, and that he himself would have dearly loved a fight, for—as I was afterwards to learn to my cost—he was not only a magnificent fighter, but did not know the meaning of fear.

The only way in which I can account for his own surrender—for only a day or so previously he had been fully prepared to fight us—is that he had just become aware of the fact that Jiand was a prisoner in our hands. He was afraid, therefore, that if he attacked us the proud old Chief might suffer, and that, on the whole, it would be wiser to appear submissive—for the moment.

But Idu warned me at the time, and again and again in the immediate future, "Jiand and Halil Khan will never rest until they have fought you again. Unless you can get a much larger force, at the very first opportunity, and almost certainly when they learn that you have at present practically no troops, they will turn and attack you. Place no reliance on their word or their oath, even though it be given on the Koran."

That same evening I learnt of a great raid that had recently been made into Persia by a section of the Yarmahommedzais, under a leader called Izzat. As an outcome of this raid hundreds of Persian ladies and children had been dragged from their homes and brought by Izzat into the Sarhad, there to be bartered as slaves. Their sufferings, both from the indignity and shame of their present state, and the hardships they must inevitably have undergone amongst their nomad captors, after the comparative luxury of their own homes, can well be imagined.

The Sarhad-dar, a well-educated and sensitive man, as well as a brave fighter, was so overcome by the picture drawn of the sufferings of these wretched women and children that he burst into tears, and sobbing like a child, pleaded with me to ignore everything else and to at once set about returning these Persians to their homes.

Strongly as my own wishes coincided with his, I knew such a course to be impossible. I had still more important things to do. Moreover, our own situation might become desperate at any moment. Although Jiand and Halil Khan, with a handful of their followers, were prisoners in my hands, their tribes were at large, and at the first suspicion of the trick that had been played on them would be on us like a swarm of bees. It must be remembered too, that Juma Khan of the Ismailzais was still at liberty, in a position to learn that we really had no troops, and might bring his men against us at any moment.

It was obvious, therefore, that I had to deal with him before I dared attempt the rescue of any Persian women, though the thought of them and their plight, and the determination to endeavour to rescue and return them to their homes at the first possible moment never left me.

The following day I decided to hold a Durbar, so gave orders that all the Sarhadi Chiefs were to be present, and that they could bring as many of their followers as they chose.

The Durbar was held on the banks of the stream, just outside the fort, and under the shade of one of the trees. We all sat on the ground, and I opened the Durbar as I thought a commissioner might do in India, though, truth to tell, I knew very little indeed about Durbars!

I explained to the Sarhadi Chiefs, Jiand, Halil Khan, Shah Sawar, and Mahommed-Hassan, that the Sirkar (literally, ruling power) was not represented in force by what they saw at Khwash. They might be interested to know, however, that some four millions of the very finest troops in the world were then fighting under the British flag in various theatres of war all over the world, and that, as surely as night follows day, Germany would be defeated, because right and might were on our side.

I explained to them collectively, as I had explained to Jiand individually, that they had been misled by German lies and propaganda into believing that Germany was winning, and also that the Germans had turned Mussulmans. I told them that it was quite the other way about, for, in point of fact, their own fellow-Mahommedans, the Turks, had really become Germans, taking their orders from their new masters, and had taken to drinking wine and to doing other acts absolutely contrary to the teachings of the Koran.

I told them that Christians never became Mahommedans, though it was easy for them to say so to secure their own ends. I also told them that I would give them a lakh of rupees for every German they could produce who had really become a follower of the Prophet. I advised them that on such matters they should look for decision to the Sherif of Mecca as their spiritual head, and that he was entirely on the British side.

They were then recommended no longer to make fools of themselves, for I had originally come to the Sarhad as their friend, and that, though they had fought against me, I was willing to let bygones be bygones and to be friends with them in the future. I also pointed out that all their interest lay in retaining the friendship of the Sirkar, for they would surely lose their country for ever if they persisted in the mad course of opposing us.

I asked them why their new friends had not helped them to oppose me, with advice if with nothing else? And, if these friends had really been sweeping victoriously on to overcome the British Raj, why they were not there with them?

Jiand, Halil Khan, Shah Sawar and Mahommed-Hassan all expressed their keen regret at what had occurred, promised that they would return to their old allegiance, and that, instead of fighting me any more, they would help me to restore order in the

Sarhad. They also promised to bring Juma Khan and his Ismailzais to book.

I then explained my plans for the immediate future. I told them of my intention to retain Khwash as a pledge for their good behaviour, and until such time as a benign Indian Government might see fit to return it to them. But I promised that I would send in a faithful report of their repentance for their past misdeeds, and of their promise to assist us in the future, and told them they might rest assured that the Government would do all that was right and fair.

The following day we marched out once more with the object of attacking Juma Khan at Galugan, leaving the head of the Reki clan (I think his name was Mirza Khan) in command of Khwash, with a few of his own tribe, and five of my nine infantry-men who could handle a rifle. Not, it will be considered, a very formidable garrison to leave in charge, but it was impossible to spare any more men.

We marched in the following order: Shah Sawar and his men were in front as advance guards, Halil Khan and the Gamshadzais on the left flank, and Jiand and his Yarmahommedzais on the right flank. Our infantry went with the baggage, and the guns and ammunition brought up the rear. The cavalry and a few infantrymen formed my personal escort.

I hoped by this arrangement to keep the various Sarhadi Chiefs well apart so that they might be unable to compare notes. My own small force was kept in the rear, and well together.

I was asked by the Raiders why I was making all these careful arrangements to protect my camels.

I replied that in war one had to be prepared to meet any emergency, and that I was not at all satisfied with what I had heard concerning the conduct of the Khan of Bampur, for there had been rumours that he might be foolish enough to try conclusions with me.

Bampur is situated in Persian Baluchistan, fully six marches away to the South of Khwash, and is overlooked by the Koh-i-Bazman. Bampur, it will be remembered, was the old capital of Baluchistan, but to-day it is only a squalid collection of mud-built huts and deserted gardens, clustered round a semi-ruined fort standing in an unhealthy, malarial district.

It was held at this date by a Baluchi Chief, apparently as cowardly as he was arrogant. The fear I expressed of his intention was to lull any possible suspicion of the Sarhadi Chiefs—nominally my prisoners—as to the formation of my battle array; but there remained a modicum of truth behind the reason given.

When we halted that night Landon, the Sarhad-dar, Idu and myself, as usual, took counsel as to the next day's movements, and finally decided to send two of Landon's spies to Bampur. Arrived there they were to tell the Khan that they had run away from us to warn him, because my mighty army, now on the march, might possibly take Bampur in its stride. In addition they were to tell him that, whilst it was true that the General commanding had given out that he was only going to march along the borders of the Bampur district in order to reach Galugan, where he intended to crush Juma Khan, they fully believed this to be only a blind, and that Bampur was to be first destroyed. Khwash itself had recently been threatened, and had only escaped destruction by surrender. It was now left in charge of five hundred of the British General's best troops, with ample supplies for a month.

It was only later on that I learned the success of this mission. The two spies arrived on a certain night at about one a.m. and did their part so well that, by two a.m., the terrified Khan had mounted his camel, and set forth for Makran.

Makran is an arid region lying along the shores of the Persian Gulf, and stretching inland for a distance of about sixty miles. It is filled with bare, dry mountains, and hills with curiously serrated edges. From the more fertile parts large quantities of dates are grown and exported.

Arrived at the headquarters of the British political officer, Colonel Dew, the Khan flung himself on his mercy, and implored him (so I have been told) not to allow General Dyer to attack him, though I have never seen Colonel Dew since to obtain an authentic account of the interview.

But this was another potential enemy cleared from our path, at any rate for the moment, and this was all that mattered to us.

On, or about, the 15th of April we continued our march towards Galugan, and on the second day came in view of the Koh-i-Bazman, an extinct volcano. This is an imposing mountain of between ten and eleven thousand feet, covered with snow and rising, a sheer, solitary peak, out of the plain.

At one point on the march Idu asked me whether I would like to see a curious hole in the ground lying only a little way off our line of route.

We turned aside for a few hundred yards, and, on a plain as flat as a billiard-table, with a surface coated with hardened clay—obviously, at one time, the bed of a lake—we came upon it. The perfectly level, smooth lips of the hole offered no suggestion that it had been excavated by human agency. On the contrary, it gave the appearance of having been punched in the ground by some tremendous force. The hole was about one hundred and fifty feet long, one hundred and twenty feet wide, and about fifty feet deep, with absolutely perpendicular sides.

Idu asked whether I could suggest any explanation of this formation, and, after examination, I admitted I had none to offer, asking him in turn whether any tradition was attached to it.

He replied that the hole had once been only half its present size, but twice as deep, and that his grandfather remembered how and when the hole was made.

The old man had told him that, one night when he was a youth, something had exploded in the sky and fallen to the earth, punching a hole one hundred feet deep in the plain. Owing to weather and climatic conditions, the sides of this hole had gradually fallen in, hence its present width and shallowness.

There can, therefore, be little doubt that an enormous meteorite fell here, and that it lies buried at the bottom of this hole. Its locality is about seven hundred yards from a hill called Gwarko, and could easily be found by anyone interested in such phenomena.

This is not the only natural feature which would repay a visit from those interested in natural science, for, though I am no geologist or scientist myself, I was greatly interested in the numerous gorges in the vicinity of Kacha, a post in the hills near Robat, where, at certain seasons of the year, violent spates occur, and the rushing water has so burnished the sides of the rocks that they glisten in the sun like polished, variegated marble. The sections so made show a close mass of fossils, which, apparently, were once oysters, centipedes, crabs, etc.

CHAPTER VI

A FULL BAG OF PRISONERS

The march to Kacha—The food supply—Flowers in the Wilderness—Galugan—Repeated strategy—Juma Khan comes in—The bag is full—The throne of the dancing maidens—Landon declines—Idu's doubts—Suspicions aroused—Halil Khan closes up—Kacha, oaths, and thumb-marks—The Chiefs depart—Bad news.

THE march from Khwash to Kacha was over constantly ascending ground, and the higher the altitude reached the more abundant did the vegetation become.

On the third day I noticed that a great many of the Raiders were carrying bunches of green stuff under their arms, plucked along the line of march, and I asked Idu what they were going to do with it.

He replied that they would eat it raw, and supplemented this information with the further news that, beyond a few dried dates, the surrendered Raiders had brought hardly any rations with them. Consequently, and very shortly, I should be called upon to feed them. This was an alarming prospect. We had left a generous supply of food behind for the garrison of Khwash, thus reducing our own rations to a bare sufficiency for the considerable distance to be covered.

I instructed Idu to ward off the evil day as long as possible, but told him that, in the last extremity, our food supplies would, of course, be fairly and evenly shared with the Sarhadis.

At this stage in the march we reached a height of some seven thousand feet, and I was struck with the beauty of the scene. Around us the slopes were covered with a profusion of flowers of every hue, forming, so it seemed, a vast, variegated carpet. Although I know nothing whatever of flowers from a botanical point of view the beauty of many of them struck me so much that, later in the year, I collected some of the seeds and preserved them carefully with the idea of home cultivation. These seeds remained with me in all my wanderings, but, unfortunately, on my journey home the pocket-book containing them was lost.

One plant in particular, the asefœtida (locally known as hing), is very striking, and most effective in the distance. The lower leaves are very big, and the plant throws up a tall, yellow shoot, two or three feet high, topped by a cluster of the most brilliant flowers of the same colour. This plant is much valued by the Baluchis, and I am told that large quantities are exported from this district to India.

We were lucky in finding cool camping places on the third and fourth nights of the march. On the

SURRENDERED RAIDERS: HALIL (left), JIAND (centre), SHAH SAWAR (right).

fifth we commenced our last march on the plain to Galugan, the territory belonging to the Ismailzais under their leader, Juma Khan.

Galugan is like Kamalabad, a district only populated during certain seasons of the year, when the Ismailzais make a regular encampment there, live in jugis, and settle down for a time to the cultivation of their crops. The place is well watered, with a very fertile soil capable of bearing magnificent crops of wheat and barley.

As we approached the camping ground of Galugan our scouts came back to inform us that Juma Khan had deserted Galugan, and had gone, with all his tribe, into the high hills surrounding the place. He had heard of the defeat of Jiand at Koh-i-taftan, of his subsequent surrender, and of the capture of Khwash. He had also seen our forces approaching, and had no hope of success if he had remained to offer battle.

As a matter of fact we really did present quite an imposing appearance by this time. Our numbers had been augmented by small groups of Jiand's and Halil Khan's men who had joined us at intervals all along the route.

We accordingly marched, without any opposition, into Galugan, and found it, as reported, absolutely deserted, with the exception of one old woman who had utterly refused to desert her crops, and was eventually discovered hiding in a field.

As the threat of destruction to his crops had been

so successful with Jiand we determined to try the same threat on Juma Khan. Accordingly, messengers were sent summoning him to surrender at once, with all his force, under a similar penalty. I told the messengers to impress upon him the fact that he and his tribe were now quite isolated, that the Gamshadzais and Yarmahommedzais had surrendered, but that they, and their leaders, had been well and generously treated, their lives and crops spared, and that the same generous treatment would be accorded to him if he delivered himself up without delay.

Very shortly he sent back a message to say that he realised he was in a hopeless position, and was quite prepared to surrender unconditionally. He also offered to restore all the plunder he had taken in the direction of Nasaratabad-sippi. But he asked for a definite guarantee that his life would be spared.

I sent back word that he need have no fear on that score. My mission was to make him see the error of his ways and to re-establish good relations between his tribe and the British; also, that he would be treated exactly as I had treated Jiand and Halil Khan.

That same evening he came into camp, with some thirty of his followers as a body-guard, and formally surrendered.

He was a somewhat different type from both Jiand and Halil Khan. Juma Khan was of medium height, and slightly built. He had a very pleasing, well-cut, high-bred face, always full of smiles and laughter, as though life were one huge joke.

Idu, who, as I have already said, knew all about the Sarhadi Chiefs and their characteristic points, said to me after I had interviewed Juma Khan, " If Juma Khan gives you his oath on the Koran he will keep it. He is well known throughout the Sarhad as a man who abides by his word. Any promise, therefore, that he makes to you he will faithfully keep."

I was especially glad that Juma Khan had come into line, and for a very good reason. The easiest route for German emissaries into Afghanistan lay through his territory. On all routes across Persia water-supply is one of the most vital considerations, the consequence being that many an otherwise convenient road had had to be abandoned owing to lack of water. Now the stream which runs from Galugan, piercing the hills and running into the Persian district of Narmashir, offers an excellent supply, so making this route an easy one for German agents—if not opposed by Juma Khan. But with Juma Khan on our side it would be practically impossible for such to get through the Sarhad. It was, therefore, my policy to treat him with special consideration. To be plain, I wished him, though an unwilling captive, to be a real convert to our interests.

All the Sarhadi Chiefs were now prisoners, but the problem arose as to the best and safest method of transporting them, and all their followers, back to Kacha, fully eighty miles distant. Our own food supplies were already running very short, yet I was obliged to promise the Raiders a fair and equal share of these. We were, therefore, immediately obliged to go on half rations.

To add to our troubles the weather was beginning to get very hot on these plains, and I well knew that, at any rate on some days—owing to water difficulties—it would be necessary to make long marches.

The first march out of Galugan proved to be heavy uphill work, our route lying up a steady, steep incline. But at night we found a suitable camping ground by the side of a stream. Here again the ground was covered by a mass of beautiful flowers. The following day we descended to the Duzd-ab plain, and had only crossed some five miles of it when a hill of such extraordinary appearance came into view that Landon and I simultaneously exclaimed. This looked for all the world like a huge mushroom with flattened dome and very thick stem—obviously a hill whose upper part was of a harder formation than the lower, thus resisting with better success the attacks of time and weather.

Idu cantered up on his pony and pointed to the hill with pride. "That, Sahib," he said, "is called the Takht-i-Jinikan" (throne of the dancing maidens).

"Why was it given that name?" I asked. "Do maidens live there alone?"

Idu grinned. " Listen, Sahib, and I will tell you the story of the Takht-i-Jinikan. On beautiful moonlight nights immortal maidens are supposed to dance on the flat top of this hill. If a young man is really very good he may climb to the top of the hill alone, while they are dancing, in the hope of obtaining a bride. But he must be very good to be sufficiently worthy to win the love of one of these immortal maidens. If he succeeds she becomes mortal, and they are married."

I asked Idu if he had met anyone who had obtained an immortal bride.

Idu smiled. " I fear there is no young man in the Sarhad good enough to be worthy of the honour! "

I persuaded Landon, who was unmarried, to climb the hill with me—but not by moonlight! On our return Idu asked Major Landon if he had seen the Jinikan.

Landon replied regretfully that he had not, but was sure it was because he had not been able to ascend the hill by moonlight—certainly not because he was not good enough. He, however, had seen some very large footprints, which he sincerely trusted, for the sake of the beauty of the legend, did not belong to these immortal damsels!

But what pleased me more than the romantic hill was the discovery of a stream only a short distance away. This afforded not only an unexpectedly good supply of water, but, from a quantity of dry bushes along its banks, an abundance of fire wood for cooking.

On each day of the march we held counsel with the Sarhadis and soon became on friendly terms with them. We found them a very interesting crowd, full of adventure and the joy of life. They informed me that, as they had now thrown in their lot with me, they were quite ready to take part in any raid with me, if only I would organise one. Nor did the objective matter. Persia, Afghanistan, or, in fact, anywhere where there might be excitement and adventurous doings. So friendly, indeed, were we all that I began to think my work, and the whole object for which I had been sent to the Sarhad, accomplished.

But Idu was never optimistic on the subject. He invariably shook his head, and warned me, in and out of season, against Halil Khan and Jiand. He, at last, so infected me with his own anxiety, that I began to wonder whether the two Chiefs might not take it into their heads to wipe out our little force one night. They could have done this with the utmost ease. This change of mind induced me at last to make my camp dispositions with redoubled care. The Raiders were given to understand that they must take part in organising the camp against some unknown foe who might make them, as well as myself, an object of attack.

My suspicions were further aroused by the minute way in which they questioned me as to the individuality of that foe, and the direction from which it would be possible for him to come. I told them that habit in soldiers becomes second nature; that it was a soldier's habit to take the utmost precaution in self-defence, and that neglected precaution might always bring possible disaster. But I could see that they accepted the explanation with doubt, and obviously disbelieved in my mythical foe.

The third day's march across the Duzd-ab valley was a very trying one. We had to make a double march, for our food supplies were almost exhausted, and it was obviously imperative to reach Kacha as soon as possible. It must be remembered, too, that we had been on half rations since leaving Galugan, and already there had been much grousing amongst the whole force.

That night we encamped at the base of a hill which Jiand proudly announced as "Koh-i-Jiand-siah," or the "Hill of Black Jiand." I asked him who Black Jiand might be, and he replied that his father's name was Jiand, though he was not black, and that the hill had been named after him. The old fellow was obviously proud of the honour which had been conferred on his father.

Here Landon and I spent an anxious night, for both Idu and the Sarhad-dar were very nervous and depressed. The latter said that a rumour had got about amongst the Sarhadis that all my promises and protestations to them were false, and that I was really leading them into a trap at Kacha, where they were all to be killed. Consequently, the idea had been discussed as to whether it might not be safer, and wiser, to attack our small force, overwhelm us during the night, and escape before daybreak.

As may be imagined, the prospect was scarcely a pleasant one, but we could take no stricter precautions than had already been done, and our sole remaining action now was to show an absolutely untroubled and confident front to men who, though nominally our prisoners, held us in the hollow of their hands. In other words to " trust to luck."

Fortunately for us the Raiders, who still could not make head or tail of the real situation, determined on a pacific course, and the night passed without incident. So luck stood with us, and on the following morning we were early astir for the last march south of Kacha.

It was evident that the situation had now become one of the " touch and go " order, so I determined to emphasise my supposed confidence in the Raiders, by this means restoring theirs, and convincing them that there was no trap. I, therefore, gave orders that none of them were to march in advance, but in the rear, as I wished to have a clear view of my covering troops.

As we drew in towards Kacha I noticed that Halil Khan and his band gathered as close in behind me as possible, and I learned afterwards that he had said, " If we are to be led into a trap I will see to it that the General Sahib does not escape me."

CAMEL CORPS SAWARS AT THE TERMINATION OF OPERATIONS.

I had already given orders that, the instant we entered Kacha, the advance guard of infantry, also the cavalry and guns, were to march straight off to their respective barracks. This order I learned afterwards greatly relieved the anxiety of the Sarhadis, who had actually talked themselves into an honest belief of the existence of a trap. They themselves encamped in the vicinity of the British Political Officer's house. He himself was absent at that date. Ample food supplies were dealt out to them. Now that our lines of communication were clear of the Raiders food was coming through again from India.

For the moment all need for anxiety seemed at an end.

On the 1st of May I summoned a Durbar, to be held, on the following day, close to the Political Officer's house. Idu was not present, for he had asked for leave to go to Robat on important personal business. I suspected this important business was a visit to one of his numerous wives, though the rascal always disclaimed the suggestion that his absences ever had anything to do with a woman.

The Durbar was an impressive affair. Several bags of money were brought from the Government Treasury by the Sarhad-dar and placed at my feet. These were to be given to the Chiefs as rewards for future good conduct. After delivering an address —more or less a repetition of what I had said at Khwash as to the folly of deserting the British for the Germans—I called on the Chiefs to sign an agreement whereby they handed their country over to the Sirkar, and promised in future to be loyal to the Indian Government. Further than this, and under this agreement, they were to give timely warning of the approach of German agents from any direction.

As most of the Raiders could not write, their thumb-marks were duly impressed on an imposing looking document produced by the Sarhad-dar, and the Chiefs swore on the Koran to abide by the agreement. They were then handed the money rewards promised them, Jiand receiving the largest amount—two thousand rupees.

I then announced to them that they were all free to return to their homes, and that if ever any of them needed a friend, or would like me to adjudicate between them on any local quarrel, they were at liberty to call upon me for the purpose.

They professed themselves as very grateful for all that had been given them; admitted they had been treated generously, and promised, on oath, that there should be no more trouble in the Sarhad, nor should any German or German agent be permitted to pass through their territories.

Thus, when they left for their homes, on the morning of May 3rd, all parties were, apparently, on excellent terms.

I wrote a despatch to headquarters at Simla, giving a short account of the expedition and its results, at the same time bringing forward the names of various officers, and other ranks, for good work done. I also mentioned the fact that I did not know what to do in regard to the traffic in slaves.

That evening Idu returned. He came straight to my room and told me I had acted unwisely in disregarding his repeated warnings as to the unreliability of Jiand and Halil Khan. He further added that some of his own chosen men, who had been scouting around and picking up all possible information, had met him, on his return to Kacha, and had given him the following authentic and disquieting news. It was to the effect that, hardly had Jiand got out of Kacha, that morning, with promises of devotion and loyalty still hot upon his lips, than he had halted and called a meeting of the Raider Chiefs, urging them to repudiate their oaths, to collect all their fighting men as quickly as possible, attack and take Khwash, and then to turn their attention to my force, which he now openly said he knew to be a contemptibly small one.

This was bad news indeed. We naturally knew that Khwash could be captured in a few minutes. There were only five men there. We were also quite conscious of the fact that we could be wiped out in less than the same time if attacked in any force.

But the bad was leavened by the good, for the same report told us that Juma Khan had resolutely and absolutely refused to fall in with Jiand's plans.

He was also reported to have said that the General Sahib had kept every promise made to them, had spared their lives and crops when he could have destroyed them, had treated them, from the commencement of hostilities, as honourable foes, and later as friends, and had finally given them considerable sums of money. He had never broken his word, and he did not intend to begin doing so now. Therefore, he was to be counted out of any plans of treachery which Jiand might be meditating. Upon which expression of opinion he had ridden off to his own country with his following.

But, even with Juma Khan eliminated, the situation was serious enough, for I saw no chance of obtaining reinforcements from any quarter in time to prevent a disaster. However, it was no use crying over spilt milk. Things must be faced as they were.

After all, as I pointed out to Idu, Jiand could not do the impossible. He and Halil Khan could not collect their scattered men in a moment. The one thing left for us to do was to set off on the morrow, march back to Khwash, endeavour to reach it before Jiand, and organise our defence against his coming.

I have often since been blamed for an apparent foolhardiness in trusting the Raiders sufficiently to let them go. But it must be remembered that I had not come out to fight the Raiders—unless events made it absolutely necessary to do so—but, rather, to make friends with them and to keep the Germans, or their agents, from coming through their country. Moreover, the force at my disposal was very small indeed, and quite insufficient to keep these Raiders in check when once the bluff was called. In other words, I should soon lose the game if I persisted in treating them as enemies.

It must be understood, too, that the Sarhad was only the Southern portion of my command, and that rumours were constantly coming in that Germans, who had failed to get through into Afghanistan via the South, were not only moving North towards Birjand, but were trying to cross the border in that direction.

I knew, also, that it would soon be necessary to move North in order to induce the Russians to keep a more careful guard than they had been doing in the district North of Birjand, a district within their sphere of influence in Persia.

Nor must it be supposed that I had not quite realised, before I let the Raiders go, that I had not obtained all the safeguards I could have wished. But I did not then, nor do I now, see that I had any other alternative.

In any case I had gained one very definite advantage. I had won over Juma Khan to our side; and it was through his territory that the Germans would first have to pass in order to get through the Sarhad.

But, though Juma Khan had already given a practical example of his determination to be loyal to his oath, I recognised that he would be bolstered up in his loyalty if he felt there was apparent some show of strength on our side. The loss of Khwash to Jiand would, therefore, be a terrible confession of weakness.

Landon and the Sarhad-dar fully concurred with me that the one and only wise plan to follow would be to march at daybreak with all the forces we could command, and endeavour, by a series of forced marches, to reach and enter Khwash before Jiand could take it.

CHAPTER VII

THE RACE FOR KHWASH

Plans and routes—Car versus legs—An equestrian interlude—The trap in the gorge—More digging—Rendezvous—Mrs Idu and gastronomy—A reinforcement—A message to Landon—Izzat's men—Idu's romance—A "British Bulldog"—The car abandoned.

TIME was obviously the chief factor to be reckoned with for any hope of ultimate success; I wondered, therefore, whether the car might not be utilised in this dash back to Khwash.

Considering the nature of the ground over which we had marched, it seemed rather a mad idea, but Idu pounced on it.

"The very thing, Sahib," he said excitedly. "You remember how astonished even I was when I first saw it? How much more will it impress Jiand's ignorant men! They will think it a new sort of devil, and it will be more useful than a dozen guns!"

"I believe Idu is right," Landon said. "Why don't you go in the car, whilst I take charge of the army?"

After further details had been discussed, we decided to adopt this plan. The car was still at

Robat, about twenty-four miles distant, with Allan in charge. I, therefore, sent a telegram, and also a duplicate message by a sawar on a mari camel, telling Allan to provision the car, bring all the spare tubes and tyres he possessed, and start early the following morning on the track to Saindak, where, at a spot to which the sawar would guide him, about nine miles out of Kacha, Idu and I would meet him on horseback.

Landon, who would be able to use a far more direct route to Khwash than the car could take, was to start with the army—the same old army of seventeen cavalrymen, four trained infantrymen (it will be remembered five had been left in Khwash), sixty-five untrained men, with two mountain guns, two machine-guns, and six hundred camels. He was to endeavour to reach the Raiders' stronghold in seven marches.

Six hundred camels for so small a force would seem out of all proportion. But it must be remembered that transport for provisions, and everything else we should need for at least a full month, was required; that we could not depend on keeping open any sort of lines of communication; and that whenever a Durbar or meeting was held, all those attending it expected to be fed, and well fed. Our very existence depended on an ample supply of food. Further, the presence of so many camels helped to uphold the game of bluff it was still necessary to play, and a distant view of these six hundred camels gave an appearance of numbers out of all proportion to our real fighting strength.

Landon's route would take him by a comparatively short cut, though, even by this—over the western slopes of the Koh-i-taftan—he could not hope to accomplish the march in less than seven days.

Very early in the morning Idu and I rode off on a couple of small ponies provided by the former, and he assured me that it was only a very special breed of pony that could hope to cope with the difficulties of the nine hilly miles lying between us and the meeting-place arranged with Allan and the car.

Idu was fully justified in his criticism of the track we had to follow, for it grew steeper and narrower as we proceeded, until, at last, we were negotiating a mere cleft in the hill, with our elbows almost touching the rocky sides.

Suddenly, my pony, who had probably been deciding that he had had enough of it, stopped dead, quivered all over and—sat down! Idu, who was immediately in front, turned round to see what had happened, and his pony promptly rolled backwards on the top of us.

I got clear as well as I could for laughing, helped Idu—who was very badly shaken—to extricate himself from the ponies, and then, between us, got the ponies out of the crevasse into which they had managed to jam themselves. This took some time, and when we got them up we found the poor beasts so frightened that we had to walk them the greater part of the way.

At eleven o'clock, perspiring from every pore, we reached the *rendezvous* arranged, and to our great relief found Allan waiting, stolid, imperturbable, reliable as ever, with the car in spick-and-span order. Poor Allan little knew what he was in for. He had, of course, seen nothing of our recent little campaign, as he had remained at Robat during the past few weeks. He was, therefore, quite delighted at the prospect of a little activity.

We gave our ponies to the camel sawars who had acted as guides to Allan, with instructions to take them back to Kacha, so Idu and I took our places, thankful to be in the car once more, and set off on our journey South.

We soon passed through Saindak, and, as the going was not quite as bad on that first day as we had expected, we got farther than we had hoped, reaching a halting place called Jujak, where there was an old ruined sarai (rest-house) and a good spring. Here we slept out in the open, and set off early on the following morning. Idu was greatly impressed with the powers of the car, and began to think it could go anywhere, scale any height, and slip through any opening, however narrow. This was flattering to the Overland, but it led us into future difficulties from which only great good luck extricated us.

We had intended going via Mirjawa, but Idu

pointed out that there was a much shorter way through the hills, which, he was quite certain, the car could manage. But we were to prove once more that the longest way round may often be the shortest way home!

The car entered the hills by a gorge which rose steeply to their summits, and, though we had to get out occasionally and push, it really was astonishing how well she took the inclines. But it was when we descended that our troubles began, for, in doing so, we entered another gorge which grew narrower and narrower, till, at last, Allan stopped the car dead, declaring that we could go no farther. And a glance at our route did seem to show that we had manœuvred ourselves into a hopeless impasse.

Ahead the gorge was too narrow to allow of going on. Behind it was so steep that the car could not back out. On the right we were completely shut in by the high steep sides of the gorge, on the left it looked as impassable; whilst it was quite impossible to turn!

There remained nothing for it but to dig a way out, so we set to work, and, after working till we were wet through, managed somehow to get the car through the wall of earth shutting us in on the left, and out on to the open hill-side.

Idu openly expressed his disgust and disappointment with the car. He had given her credit for being capable of doing anything and going anywhere, and this failure to pass through " the eye of a needle " diminished his respect for her.

There was still no direct way down the hill, and we had perforce to go many miles out of our course, in a long hair-pin loop, to reach anything like decent going. No one who has not attempted to take a car over trackless hills of rough, broken surface, and filled with blind gorges, can have any idea of the difficulties that confronted us here, and during the greater part of our journey to Khwash.

By dint of ceaseless pulling and pushing, and digging the car out again and again, we managed to reach the *rendezvous* with Landon before nightfall. He marched in a few minutes after we arrived, and was as frankly pleased as astonished to see us. He had just come through another section of those hills himself. He had not, therefore, expected the car would get through, and was wondering how on earth I should ever rejoin him and the army. So we all camped out in the open, grateful for the coolness of the evening, for the heat of the day had been terrific.

Before sunrise on the following morning Landon marched out, and, as soon as we had lost sight of him, Idu, Allan, and myself set off in the car.

I do not propose to give a detailed account of the remainder of our journey. One day was very like another, and the bad surface only differed in quality and degree. The heat was very great by day, and the glare over the sandy wastes and hills almost blinding. Here and there, especially in the Galugan valley, we came across groups of human beings, mostly of a low type of humanity, who bolted in terror at sight of the car.

One evening we halted at a settlement of Rekis, Idu's own tribe, and received a very warm welcome, for one of Idu's wives was amongst his people. The rascal always maintained that he had no interest in women, but, nevertheless, seemed to me to be a very good understudy to the proverbial sailor, for he appeared to have a wife in every village and encampment.

This particular Mrs Idu was delighted at the unexpected reunion with her husband, and did the honours of the camp right royally. Following accepted custom, I, first of all, bought a few sheep from the Jugi-dwellers, and then presented these to them so that they could prepare a feast. Mrs Idu, a very unprepossessing-looking, but highly amiable lady, acted as hostess, and we all squatted round the camp fires while the meat was roasting.

Allan's face was a picture as he watched the tribesmen cook and eat their meat. They hacked chunks of flesh from the dead carcasses of the sheep with the knives they always carried, spitted them on the cleaning rods of their rifles, and roasted them over the fire. These they ate voraciously, as though very hungry, and, as a matter of fact, food in that district is both scarce and monotonous. In any case they devoured the meat whilst it was still nearly raw. Even Idu ate his meat half-cooked, maintaining that it was far more tender in such a state.

Of course, the car was a source of intense interest and excitement. At first the tribesmen were too afraid of it to go anywhere near it, but when they saw it stand quite still at Allan's orders, and that it had no bite, curiosity overcame fear, and, one by one, they crept up and nervously touched it. At this stage Allan sounded the Claxton, and, with shrieks of terror, they all bolted. But Idu, who had come over the mountains in it, and, therefore, had lost all fear of the monster, felt a devil of a fellow, and, with a flourish, assured them it was not the roar inside which made it go, and that it would do no one any harm. So they came back to it once more, and, after some persuasion, were induced to sound the Claxton themselves. Once familiar with it, they laughed like children each time it barked, and I began to wish I had taken the thing off before we started.

After supper Idu prepared my blankets under the shelter of a small bush, but, before turning in, I sat down on the ground for a final smoke, placing the hurricane lamp from the car on the hard smooth earth in front of me.

The light naturally attracted myriads of insects of all sorts, many of which I had never seen before, and which are, I feel sure, unknown in India. Beetles of many sorts swarmed around, both in the air and on the ground, whilst a scorpion, the biggest

I have ever seen, darted out from the darkness to inspect the light. He was a brown fellow, not an iridescent blue, like the Burmese variety, though he was quite as big. With his tail curled right over his back, and sting ready to strike, he looked a formidable person, and it was comic to watch the haste with which all the lesser fry scuttled out of his way, and, though he made many attempts to secure his supper, I did not see him succeed, so swift were his intended victims in escaping from their dreaded enemy.

We were, as usual, up in the morning before daybreak, and en route before the rest of the camp was astir. The going that morning proved fairly good, the chief obstacle being huge clumps of a coarse, rank grass, which we had to circumvent.

We had proceeded some distance when Idu, whose eyes seemed able not only to see in the dark, but through hills and fields of crops, suddenly exclaimed, " I can see men in front of us. We had better halt while I go forward and find out whether they are friends or enemies."

We stopped the car, for we were now on the borders of Jiand's territory, and these men might be his followers treating us to an ambush. Idu leapt out, and, advancing under cover with the eel-like movements all these Raiders possess, reconnoitred the position. Obviously all was well, for, shortly afterwards, he sauntered back in the open and told me that it was quite all right. The men he had seen were Rekis, and they were now coming to speak to me.

Soon afterwards fifteen well-armed, powerful-looking men on camels ambled up to us, and I was grateful indeed to know they were friendlies and not Jiand's men.

They, however, kept at a respectful distance from the car, which was still retaining its moral effect, and implored me, as the friend and protector of Idu and of themselves, to go back.

" Jiand is advancing on Khwash, Sahib, with a big lashkar," they said. " He is probably already there, and he will kill you and your followers unless you run away on the devil which has brought you here."

I expressed a hope that their information was wrong, and that, as it was not certain that Jiand was already in Khwash, I still hoped to get there first. I pointed out to them that if we could only get into Khwash we could, with their help, hold it or even bluff Jiand into surrendering without a fight. After a little further persuasion by Idu—who told them what wonders the car could do, and what rewards they would gain—and after considerable talk among themselves they decided to throw in their lot with us.

" We shall want all the help they can give us with the car," Idu whispered to me, " for the ground we have to pass through between here and Khwash is far worse than anything we have crossed yet."

I could imagine nothing worse than the first two

days amongst the hills. But Idu knew what he was talking about, as we were to discover during the next twenty-four hours.

At this point I sent one of these men back to try and find Landon and the army. As Idu had sketched out the best route for them to follow he was able to tell him the exact direction in which to go. In the interval I wrote a message to Landon urging him to use his best speed, for it had now developed into a race between Jiand and ourselves, and telling him that I hoped to reach Khwash myself before the following evening.

I of course knew that nearly everything hung upon getting to Khwash first. If Jiand got in with his men, he could hold it as long as he chose against us, and vice versa. It was clear, too, that the holder of Khwash was master of the Sarhad. Moreover, I felt a grave responsibility for the lives of the five Sepoys I had left there, for they would meet with short shrift at Jiand's hands.

The message dispatched, we set off once more, with our new cavalcade in attendance, and had gone some twenty or twenty-five miles when Idu again asked for a halt as he believed he saw men camped in a little nullah straight ahead of us. Were he correct they would be Yarmahommedzais, and so our enemies, for we were now right in the heart of Jiand's territory.

Allan was, therefore, directed to drive the car into the mouth of a nullah close at hand, where the car, and the Rekis with their camels, could be concealed, and where we could fill up our water-bottles and the radiator, from a small stream that trickled through it. The banks of the nullah had been hollowed out by the action of the water, so affording a certain amount of shade, for which we were very grateful after the burning heart of the open sandy plain.

After rest and a drink Idu went out to reconnoitre, and presently returned with a glum face.

" They are Izzat's men," he said. (Izzat, it will be remembered, had been the ringleader in the recent raid into Persia, which had resulted in the capture of so many women and children). " Izzat is a great fighter, and we are in for a scrap."

" How many men has he with him? " I asked.

" About eighteen," Idu replied.

" Only eighteen? " I felt relieved. " Why, then we are about equal in numbers, to say nothing of the car. If they want a fight they shall have it."

Idu looked dubious. " In any case it would mean the loss of many of my tribe, and we shall want them all if we are to hold Khwash. Will the General Sahib permit me to go and see if I can persuade Izzat not to fight? "

Knowing Idu's persuasive qualities I gave a ready consent, but warned him to take no personal risks. With his great knowledge of the country, and of all the Sarhadis with their different peculiarities, he was absolutely indispensable to me, and I have no hesitation in making the admission. Furthermore, I had conceived a very genuine affection for the man, whose utter devotion and loyalty never swerved from the moment he joined me.

"Have no fear, Sahib," he said with a grin. "You know the law of our tribes. It is the one law we never break."

Idu then went forward, and, from safe cover, shouted out to Izzat, explaining who he was, and asking for a safe conduct. This was instantly given.

I have said before in this narrative, and I proved again and again, that whilst the Raiders would break every other law and oath, even when given on the Koran, the one law they never break is that of hospitality. If they promise safe conduct it is absolutely observed in letter and spirit.

Accordingly, Idu went forward boldly, quite certain, according to the code of his enemies, that his life was safe until he returned to his friends.

His conversation with Izzat proved a lengthy one. Izzat was hard to convince. But, at last, and as usual, Idu's wily tongue won the day. When he returned it was to tell me that he had persuaded Izzat and his men to come along with us, if not as friends at any rate not as enemies.

He gave me a *résumé* of the arguments he had used. These were original, even for Idu, with whose methods I was beginning to be familiar. The conversation must have been something as follows:

"What are you doing here, Izzat? Your home is a long way from here."

" I have come to fight the British General, and I am in command of a reconnoitring party to report to Jiand, who is advancing on Khwash."

" Do I understand you? " said Idu. " Do you seriously mean that you have come with the intention of fighting the General Sahib? "

" I do," replied Izzat.

" Then," said Idu scornfully, " all I can tell you is that you will be wiped out in a couple of seconds. If you fight, you will prove yourself a liar. The General Sahib captured you and could have killed you and all your men. Instead he treated you well, gave you back your rifles, large sums of money, and let you go free. Moreover, you swore on the Koran at Kacha that you would never fight against him again, and put your thumb-mark on the agreement. You are a fine kind of Mahommedan to break your oath given on the Koran. Besides, you fool, don't you know that the General Sahib has brought a wonderful devil with him? Come over here and look."

He led Izzat to a spot whence he could see the car.

" Do you see," he went on, " that queer thing there? And do you see that the front part of it is filled with hundreds of little holes? The General Sahib has only to press a button and a hail of bullets will come out of those holes, and you, and all your men, will be killed. He is only waiting till I go back. I have come out to try and save your lives. If I tell him that you are going to fight he will press the button, and there will not be one of you left. Your only hope is to go and fall at his feet and ask him to forgive you."

Izzat was deeply impressed, and, after consultation with his men, told Idu that he would accept his advice. If, therefore, he would go back and beg the Sahib not to destroy them with his motor-car they would follow a few minutes later and surrender!

Allan roared with laughter at Idu's explanation of the radiator, but after a few moments grew serious.

"Do you think it's safe to let them come, sir? They seem a pretty brutal lot; and when they find out that Idu has been spoofing them they may attack us, and cut our throats before we can do them much damage?"

"I know, but we'll hang on to Idu's bluff about the radiator as long as we can. Besides, we are nearly man to man. Remember, the one thing to do is to show no sign of fear or doubt of them. That impresses them more than anything."

So Allan and I remained seated in the shade of the overhanging bank, whilst Izzat and his men came and sat in a circle in front of us. I then proceeded to tell Izzat, in very plain language, what I thought of him.

His mind was still visibly working under the impression Idu had produced, for he appeared quite cowed in his apologies for his conduct.

After a long dressing-down I thought it advisable to make a show of magnanimity, so promised to forgive him on condition that he and his men came along with me, and helped me when I needed assistance with the car. I explained that, though it was a devil, yet the sand sometimes obstructed it and then it needed human help.

Izzat promised anything and everything I asked, even volunteering to fight for me if I wanted him.

This latter promise, however, I utterly discounted. It was not in the least likely that he would fight against his own tribe, and I knew that we should have to be perpetually on the look-out for treachery, especially until Landon and his little force arrived.

But I had got out of Izzat, whilst still uncertain of his fate, the information that Jiand's preparations for the taking of Khwash had been quicker than I had expected; also that he was already on the march in full force, and would surely reach Khwash the following day.

This meant that we had not a moment to lose. I had hoped that by arriving on the following evening I should be in time. But now we must make a dash for it, and, by hook or by crook, arrive by the morning.

Evening was already approaching, but instead of camping for the night as I had intended, and getting by daylight through the hills lying between us and the valley in which Khwash stood, it would now be necessary to negotiate them by night.

Allan looked dubious when I told him of my decision.

"I can't guarantee to get the car through, sir," he said. "Idu says these hills are far worse than the hills near Ladis, and you know what a job we had getting through them by daylight. But I'll do my best."

And if ever a man did his best Allan did his right nobly that night.

A whole series of hills, without any tracks over them, intersected with nullahs, valleys filled with sand-drifts, and marshy tracts, had to be negotiated in the darkness, lighted only by the stars and the car's lamps.

On the lower slopes we got stuck again and again in the narrow steep-sided nullahs, and it took the combined efforts of the Rekis, Izzat's men and a stout rope, always carried on the car, to drag her out. Over and over again it seemed as though we must give up the attempt and wait for daylight. But Allan came of the right stock. He also knew well how vitally important for British prestige throughout the Sarhad it was to be first in Khwash, and so confirm our supremacy there.

So Allan stuck to his job, muttering repeatedly, when the difficulties seemed insuperable, "I'm a British bull-dog, sir, and I am not going to be beat."

This expression of Allan's afterwards became a saying amongst our men when any difficulty arose.

But if Allan wasn't beaten the car very nearly was at one point when negotiating the worst bit of ground I have ever passed over in my life—for there was no going round it. The strata here were up-ended, and consisted of alternate layers of shale and quartz. Weathering had done its work more easily on the shale, hence the quartz, which was much thinner than the shale, projected upwards in great dagger-like points in every direction, and over a long distance.

Of course tyres and tubes were cut to ribbons in a few minutes, and, as it would have been futile to replace them, the car was literally dragged over the ground on her rims.

As may be imagined, when we had left this awful bit of ground behind, my poor car was in a pitiable condition. Luckily, Allan had plenty of spare tubes and four fresh tyres. With these adjusted, we started again, but the ground was still so bad that every mile or so we were badly punctured, and tubes had to be replaced or patched. It must be understood, too, that the heat was intense, even at night time. I can safely say that that one night's journey was the very worst I have ever experienced in any part of the world.

We were all utterly exhausted long before day-break, and, every now and again, despite our desperate anxiety, eyelids closed and heads nodded. As for Allan, sturdy bull-dog though he was, nature was too strong for him.

Just as dawn broke his heavy eyelids closed for a second as he sat at the wheel. But that second proved fatal. The car swerved a fraction from the course we had been following by the light of the lamps, and, in an instant, it was over the edge of the track and firmly embedded in a sandy nullah-bed.

A few minutes later the sun rose over the plain below us, lighting up the walls of Khwash, a bare five miles away.

Allan was in despair at the position of affairs and cursed himself for his momentary relaxation. But the damage had been done, and, as we knew by experience how long it would take to extricate the car, we decided to abandon it and press forward to Khwash with all speed.

I invited myself on to Izzat's own camel, as it looked the most comfortable! Allan was induced to get on to another, and Idu invited himself on to the next best-looking animal.

I ordered Izzat to ride close beside me, for I did not trust him for a moment, more especially since the failure of the car, whose first impression had been so satisfactory. And then, as fast as we could urge the animals, we ambled on towards our " Mecca," with the question ever before us, " shall we be in time or has Jiand forestalled us? "

CHAPTER VIII

KHWASH AND THE SECOND SURRENDER

Doubts dispelled—Organisation for defence—Idu's "Exiat"—And its result—Jiand arrives—Idu's second visit—The Sarhad-dar arrives—Landon at last—Jiand's visit of ceremony—The Gul-Bibi—Shah Sawar's treachery—We call on the "Rose Lady"—A carpet and the Sarhad-dar's advice—Another Durbar—Returned loot—Temporary peace.

As we approached the fort, still in doubt as to whether Jiand occupied it or not, Allan turned round on his camel and asked, "Which way shall we run, sir, if we have to run?"

I laughed, though I could not help approving his foresight. "There's no more running, Allan. If Jiand is not in Khwash, all will be well. If he is—well, you can take it from me, the game's up. There'll be no running for any of us."

We were now near enough to see a man standing on the top of one of the towers. Was he one of the men I had left, or a Yarmahommedzai? A few minutes later we could distinguish his uniform.

We were in time! We should be first into Khwash after all!

In my joy I took off my helmet and waved it to show the man I was not one of the enemy, for he might easily have mistaken us, seeing that we were all mounted on camels. He paused a moment, then, recognising the signal, tore down from the tower, quitted the walls and rushed out to meet us, nearly beside himself with excitement and relief.

"You are only just in time, Sahib," he said. "Shah Sawar has already arrived with a large force and is encamped close by. We have been expecting him to attack all the morning. Come quickly into the fort, or, even now, you may be too late."

We needed no second bidding, but, urging the camels forward, pressed on, and were soon all safely contained within strong mud walls.

Without a moment's delay the place was organised for defence. This was done as well as it was possible to do, pending the arrival of Landon with his force.

The five infantrymen till now constituting the garrison were put in the highest tourelle, where I also took up my quarters. From this vantage-point I not only had the best view of the whole plain but could command every inch of the fort's interior. Idu's men manned the three remaining tourelles, whilst Izzat's band were placed, all together, in the centre of the Square, where a watchful eye could be kept on them. Izzat himself I kept close by my side, for Idu, who knew him too well to trust him a yard, advised me to keep a close personal watch on him.

The place was now as secure as our limited

numbers could make it, and no more could be done but await developments.

Idu, who had never left my side, now asked permission to leave the fort for the purpose of questioning the Khwashis outside the walls. He also asked for some money with which to bribe them.

" A very little will open their mouths, Sahib," he he said persuasively. " And they will surely know all about the movements of Shah Sawar and of Jiand."

As no enemy had yet appeared in sight I gave him leave to go, and all the money I had in my pocket.

On his return he informed me that he had learned exactly where Shah Sawar and his men were encamped, and proposed that he should go out and confer with him.

At first I refused point-blank. Idu could not go on bearing a charmed life, and Shah Sawar was a treacherous scoundrel. I pointed out that even if Shah Sawar did not kill him he might take and keep him prisoner, and I could not possibly do without him. His loss would be irreparable.

Idu was obviously pleased and flattered at my appreciation of him, but persisted that his was the wiser plan.

" You have seen, again and again, Sahib, that what I have told you is always true. No Sarhadi will break his oath of safe conduct to an enemy."

" I know," I replied. " But you have not got

that promise from Shah Sawar, and without it I will not let you go."

Idu, who had the utmost faith in his own powers of persuasion, was not to be done. He argued that it would be easy enough to bribe one of the Khwashis, encamped outside, to go over to Shah Sawar and get the necessary safe conduct.

At last, and with great reluctance, I consented, provided Shah Sawar sent every assurance and guarantee that there would be no treachery if Idu went as an emissary.

In due course these assurances arrived. I had, therefore, to keep my word to Idu, and give my consent, though, even then, I did not trust Shah Sawar. However, once again Idu's confidence in that one, all-sacred law of hospitality was justified.

From my tower I watched him start, but he was very quickly lost to view amongst the sand dunes and fields with their tall-grown crops which lay between the fort and Shah Sawar's camp, some three miles distant.

He was away something like three hours, and I was beginning to get desperately anxious, when, to my great relief, I saw him ambling back on his Mari.

He was highly pleased with the success of his mission, and gave me a full and detailed account of his meeting with Shah Sawar. As usual he had taken a high tone, and, on arriving at the camp, had immediately and scornfully approached the Chief.

" So I see you are about to make a fool of yourself again. But what do you think you are going to do? The General Sahib is in Khwash waiting for you! "

At first Shah Sawar refused to believe this, saying that it was impossible to have got there from Kacha in the time. It was evident that the Khwashi sent as a messenger had faithfully kept the oath Idu had exacted from him, i.e., that he would give Shah Sawar no indication whatever of my presence, or any reason for Idu's request for a safe conduct to his camp.

But when Idu persisted that, possible or not, I was there with a considerable force, and that a large army was approaching to reinforce me, and would be in Khwash at any minute, Shah Sawar asked how on earth it had been done. He well knew the country lying between Kacha and Khwash, and he could not believe the distance had been covered since he himself had seen the General Sahib in Kacha.

Idu replied that it was nevertheless true, and that he had come in a motor-car, also that he, Idu, had come in it too!

" What is a motor-car? " asked Shah Sawar, " and how could it come over the hills? "

" A motor-car," replied Idu (this is his own account), " is an infernal machine which climbs any hill as fast as you like. It can spread bullets in every direction. Neither you nor anyone else has the slightest chance if you try to fight against it."

It appears that Shah-Sawar did not know whether

to believe or disbelieve Idu's strange statements, so produced a Koran which all Sarhadis carry concealed somewhere under their robes.

" Will you swear on the Koran that the General Sahib is in Khwash, and that he really came over the hills in this strange thing which you call a motor-car, also that this motor-car is at Khwash? "

Idu grinned when he told me that he had sworn to all these facts. " Of course I knew, Sahib, that we had left the motor-car away up in the sandhills, but I know how you loved it, and I guessed that you would have sent parties of Khwashi to fetch it in."

This is exactly what I had done under Allan's guidance, for he had been heartbroken at the thought of leaving the car to become derelict. She had therefore been dragged out by the docile Khwashis, and had only a short time before been brought triumphantly into the fort.

" Well, is Shah Sawar coming to attack us? " I queried.

" No, Sahib. He is coming, it is true, but when he comes, he will speak fair, he will pretend that he never meant to fight against you, but that he only came out with his men to do you honour! "

So in due course Shah Sawar arrived, and when Idu brought me word that he was approaching, I went outside the fort to meet him. I had not the slightest desire that he should see how few men were inside the walls, neither did I wish him to have the chance of speech with any of Izzat's men. He was received with all the dignity I could muster, and I outwardly accepted his assurance that he had only come on a friendly mission, in fact for the purpose of doing me honour. I told him, however, that for the present he must remain with me as my prisoner—or guest—anyhow until his over-lord, Jiand, had arrived and vouched for his permanent good conduct. I then asked him casually when he expected Jiand to arrive.

He replied that the old Chief would be outside the walls of Khwash that evening, and that he was then only a very few miles distant.

I then dismissed Shah Sawar under escort, and ordered Idu to select one of his trustiest men. This man I told to choose the swiftest camel in the place, to set off at once, find our approaching force, and give a letter to Major Landon. In this letter I asked Landon to send on the cavalry at once, at whatever time the message reached him, as they must, without fail, be in the fort that night or early next morning if the situation was to be saved. The infantry and supply camels must follow as soon after as possible without the protection of the cavalry.

These orders were sent because I knew perfectly well that, at any moment, our true strength, or rather our weakness, might be betrayed by some ignorant Khwashi, or worse still, by some unsuspected traitor within the walls. It does not need much imagination to understand that if Jiand had got to know the truth before reinforcements could reach us, he and Shah Sawar's men combined, would have been able to take the fort in a very short time.

Just at nightfall, to our dismay, we learned that Jiand himself, with a large following, had arrived in the immediate neighbourhood, had camped close at hand, and was preparing to attack us at once.

Once again Idu volunteered to do a conjuring trick. It was a race now against time. If Landon could reach us during the night we could snap our fingers at Jiand. If he failed, well—we were done. To gain time, even a few hours, meant everything.

So having, as usual, obtained the promise of safe conduct, Idu went out to visit Jiand, and to endeavour once more to play the great game of bluff.

But when he returned he seemed very doubtful as to the success of his mission. He told Jiand that I was already in Khwash, having arrived by motor-car, on whose supernatural powers he enlarged once more; also that my whole army was in Khwash, having come in motor-cars, which were quite wonderful, though not so wonderful as mine (Idu's powers of imagination were on the up grade!). Jiand was, moreover, acquainted with the fact that Shah Sawar had already seen the folly of attempting to fight, and had paid me a visit of ceremony and of submission. Idu went on to say that I had heard of his treachery, and the fact that he was marching towards Khwash to attack me there; also that I was in a towering rage about it, and was fully prepared for him. His urgent advice to him (Jiand) was that he should present himself at the fort at eleven o'clock the following morning, make his profound apologies to the General Sahib, and that, meanwhile, he would himself plead with the General not to be too severe with the Chief when he came to surrender!

"Do you think he'll wait till then?" I asked.

"I don't know, Sahib," Idu replied. And for once his cheery good spirits seemed to have deserted him. "I am not at all sure that Jiand believed a word I said. If he did not he will attack us to-night, and——" he stopped significantly.

We all understood. Here were we, a mere handful of men, in that old mud fort (which meant so much to both sides) with two large enemy camps outside. Either of them, if they once learned the truth, could obliterate us in a few hours. Combined, our chances would not be given even that amount of rope.

It was a desperately anxious night. Everything now depended upon Landon getting my message. If an accident, or any other untoward happening, held up his force, or delayed it, we might reckon that all was up. We could not hope to rely on bluff beyond the following morning. Some of the Khwashis would, as certain as to-morrow's sun, be questioned by the Yarmahommedzais, and, if so, the truth as to the fort's garrison would be dragged from them.

I warned the five infantrymen of the great danger threatening us, and told them that there could be no sleep for anyone that night. Everyone must keep his eyes skinned for any movement in the darkness which might be the forerunner of a sudden night attack.

I myself made no attempt to sleep, but continually patrolled to see that every man was awake and in his place, and that no movement or talking occurred amongst Izzat's men.

Interminable though it seemed, the night at last wore itself out, and, as the dawn broke, I climbed to the top of the highest tourelle, like Sister Anne, to see if anybody was coming.

So far not a sign of the army, which must approach from the North. My spirits sank, and I anxiously turned towards the East, and South-East, on which sides Jiand's and Shah Sawar's men were encamped. No signs of movement there, but this meant little, for I knew that, under cover of those well-grown crops, their men could stealthily approach, almost to the walls, before being observed.

Once again my eyes turned to the North.

The hours went by, and with every one that passed my anxiety grew. What had happened to Landon? Had he been able to make good time, or was he, as he easily might be, if anything had gone wrong, still a day's march away?

Suddenly I saw a small cloud of dust stirring in the plain to the North, and my heart bounded.

Out of the cloud of dust there presently emerged the solitary figure of a camel with a man on his back. The camel devoured the plain until it was close to the walls, and I rushed down to the gate to see who the rider might be.

It was my friend the Sarhad-dar, and I was more touched than words can express by the manner in which he met me, embarrassing though it was at the moment. He flung his arms round me and embraced me with the utmost affection, for he said that he had not hoped to see me alive. My urgent message had reached Landon, who was now pushing forward at his utmost speed. They had also had numerous confirmations of the information I had given as to the numbers Jiand was bringing against Khwash, and of his intention to retake and kill its defenders. The Sarhad-dar's early arrival was explained by his action in telling Major Landon he could not wait to ride at the slower pace of the army, but must forge on ahead to see whether he could do anything to help me. The Sarhad-dar's action was one of great bravery, for he rode quite alone through territory which he was fully aware might have been swarming with enemies, and who were actually only a short distance from his path.

When he saw Shah Sawar he turned and cursed him volubly, telling him he was an accursed liar and traitor, and that, one day, he would see to it that he got his full deserts.

Once again I mounted to the tourelle, and this time the dust raised by the approaching cavalry could be plainly seen.

Idu, who was with me, looking in the opposite direction, announced that men were moving in Jiand's camp. But, though I have very good eyesight, and though I looked hard and long in the direction indicated, I could see nothing. Idu's sight was certainly phenomenal, but he could not tell whether this movement foretold an attack or a friendly visit. In any case it was very lucky that Landon's relieving force was so close at hand.

A few minutes later Landon himself arrived with the cavalry, hot, fagged out, and covered with sand, but much bucked at the fact that he had arrived in time. The camels and infantry were only a short distance behind, for, as we knew by bitter experience, the last stage of the route had been so bad, that, until the plain had been reached, five miles away, the cavalry could make no better going than the rest of our small force; hence the short distance separating them.

As a matter of fact the whole force arrived very soon after, full of fighting spirit, despite the fact that, for over a month, it had been continually on the march.

I felt we could now snap our fingers at Jiand.

As may be imagined it was a very cheery morning, for, now that the guns had arrived, we knew that Jiand had about as much chance of taking Khwash as of grasping the moon. We had beaten him in the race with only an hour or two to spare, but since we had won, the game was up for Jiand, at any rate for the moment—and he knew it!

In due course the old ruffian, for he was not lacking in pluck whatever he might lack in truth, arrived to pay a ceremonial visit, which he said was merely for the purpose of doing me honour. He had heard, he said, that it had been represented to the General Sahib that he had come on a warlike mission. This rumour was quite untrue. He had merely come, with about a hundred of his tribe, to repeat the assurances he had already given of his absolute loyalty to the British Raj! As a matter of fact he had left the bulk of his men at the camp because he was afraid that they would be disarmed.

He then asked whether he might see the motor-car, about which he had heard such wonderful stories. I promptly deputed Idu the romancer as lecturer, for no one could compete with him in a description of its marvels.

Allan solemnly set the car in motion, and Jiand and his men gazed at him as a sort of demi-god. So one must be who could so control the devil in this queer shaped thing that he could make it, without the help of camels or horses, move across the plain and climb the hills. Both he and the General Sahib must surely be in close league with Sheitan!

After a while I asked Jiand if he would like to go for a ride in it, assuring him he would enjoy it. But he promptly replied that he would not risk it that day. Perhaps at some other time.

As a matter of fact the old Chief was utterly unnerved at his second failure, and obviously under the impression that his position as over-lord of the Sarhad was once again in jeopardy.

When Jiand left I gave Shah Sawar leave to go too, but warned him that the next time he broke his word it would be the last chance he would get of doing it.

Towards evening Idu, who had slipped away from the fort on secret business of his own, came up to my quarters to tell me that when Jiand and Shah Sawar had got back to their camp, they had received a fine scolding from the Gul-Bibi, Shah Sawar's wife, for whose fair sake, it will be remembered, the latter had bartered Khwash to Mahommed-Hassan, her nearest male relation.

And he chuckled as he went on to describe how this imperious lady had jeered at them both, calling them fools, and twitting them with the fact that it was now common talk that the General had arrived with a mere handful of men, and had simply tricked them into surrender. Nor did she leave the matter there. She proceeded to tell Jiand that, had he had the heart of a mouse he could have attacked and taken Khwash the night before, or even early that morning, for the General's little force had not arrived till the sun was well up.

For her part, she said all her admiration was for the General, and she intended to send him two sheep as a present, and as a mark of her appreciation.

" As a matter of fact," Idu concluded, " the sheep have already arrived."

" But I can't accept presents from a people who have been showing themselves hostile," I said. " And how is it that a woman can have the audacity to lecture a Chief like Jiand, whatever she may do to her own husband? "

" You don't know the Gul-Bibi—yet," Idu grinned. " But you will. She is one of the most influential individuals in the Sarhad, though she is a woman. Also, she is one of the most beautiful women in the world. And you must pardon me, Sahib, but you must accept the sheep she has sent. For it would be looked upon as a great insult were you to refuse."

The Sarhad-dar concurred, saying that there was no choice. The sheep must be accepted as a peace-offering.

I gave in, and asked what I ought to do in return.

" Go and call upon her, Sahib," said Idu. " The Gul-Bibi is accustomed to have honour paid to her."

" All right," I replied, and turning to Landon, who had been present and much amused, I added, " You'll have to come too. I'm a married man, and I'm not going to call on the most beautiful woman in the world alone; though, by the way, I suppose she will be veiled? "

" Certainly not," Idu put in. " The Gul-Bibi values her good looks far too highly to conceal them. I'll let her know to-night that you and Major Landon will call upon her to-morrow in the motor-car. She will be more pleased at that than at the gift of many sheep."

That evening Landon gave me a very disconcerting piece of information, particularly so in the light of present arrangements. It was to the effect that, on the way to Khwash, he had captured one of Shah Sawar's men carrying letters to the Germans. These letters had been written immediately after Shah Sawar had been released from Kacha, and in the face of the promises given and oaths sworn on the Koran. In these letters he had renewed his offers of help, and had undertaken to allow them to pass, whenever they chose, through his section of the Sarhad.

" The treacherous brute! " I exclaimed. " What on earth are we to do about him now? I've just sent him back to his own people, and have come to terms with Jiand. Moreover, we have accepted the Gul-Bibi's peace offering, and have promised to visit her to-morrow. She seems so influential, too, that if we make friends with her, these ruffians may really keep their word this time."

After considerable discussion we decided to ignore Shah Sawar's treachery for the present and proceed as arranged.

Shah Sawar and Jiand had large numbers of their fighting men on the spot, and Halil Khan, with a third big force, was to be expected on the morrow. We must, therefore, endeavour to disperse some of these brigands to their homes before we court-martialled that arch-villain Shah Sawar!

The following morning Landon, the Sarhad-dar, Idu and myself, set off in the car to call upon the Rose Lady—the most beautiful woman in the world!

Half-way there Shah Sawar himself came to meet us, and eventually conducted us to a huge jugi. Inside this we found the famous beauty, seated on a pile of coloured cushions. To my great surprise I found that Idu had not exaggerated. The Gul-Bibi really was a beautiful young woman, very fair for a Sarhadi, with regular, clean cut, almost Grecian features, and unusual-looking, big hazel eyes. She was evidently small-boned, and her limbs and hands were beautifully modelled. She was obviously aware of her own attractions, and very animated. Her dress was white, embroidered in Persian colourings, and she wore a chuddah over her head, which fell in graceful folds, without, however, in any way concealing her face.

On our entry she rose with dignity and bowed. Shah Sawar then proceeded to introduce us one by one. We each bowed in turn, and, at her invitation, sat on the ground in front of her, in a semicircle.

She then proceeded to make us a very charming address in Persian, which Landon and I understood, though we could neither of us speak much Persian. This concluded, with the Sarhad-dar's help, as interpreter, I did my best to make a suitable reply.

These preliminaries completed, a very beautiful

Persian carpet was produced and offered to me by our hostess.

This was very embarrassing, and I whispered to the Sarhad-dar that I could not possibly accept it.

His reply was emphatic. " You cannot refuse it. You must accept it as you have come here as her guest."

" But," I persisted, " I've got to court-martial her husband to-morrow, or the next day, and shall probably have to shoot him. I can't take a present from her under such circumstances."

" Shoot him, then, if you must," replied the Sarhad-dar. " She can get plenty of husbands. But you must accept the carpet now or you will give dire offence. You can in any case send a money present of equivalent value to-morrow if you like."

So I was obliged to accept the carpet with the best grace I could, and did my best in halting Persian to praise both the gift and the giver.

After this the interview proceeded merrily, and the Gul-Bibi proceeded to chaff her husband quite openly, telling him that he had been cleverly tricked and scored off. She also told him that he was a fool and as one without intelligence.

But Shah Sawar only laughed, taking his wife's raillery in good part. It was obvious that she had him very much under her thumb, and that he had a very strong regard for her.

Altogether it resolved itself into quite a friendly meeting, and, presently, we adjourned to inspect the car, which, as usual, was the occasion of much awe and wonderment. The inspection over we invited the Gul-Bibi to go for a ride in it one day, after which we took our leave and made our way back to Khwash.

A day or so later Halil Khan arrived with a following of about twenty-five men. He had left his lashkar some miles away, for he had, of course, heard of the surrender of both Jiand and Shah Sawar. Immediately upon his arrival we held another Durbar, and around the circle sat the same old collection of warriors, with their Chiefs Jiand, Shah Sawar, Mahommed-Hassan and Halil Khan. Juma Khan, the only man of his word I had yet encountered, was the one absentee.

Those who were present all solemnly swore to the fact that they were there on an entirely friendly mission, and that, if I had suspected otherwise, I had been totally misinformed! They were all sucking doves, or their equivalent, whose one desire was to do me honour!

I played up to the game, accepted their protestations, and told them that, this being so, I had a proposition to make. I then proceeded to suggest that the Chiefs, each with a certain number of followers, should remain with me, whilst the remainder were sent back to their homes. My idea, I said, was to raise a corps of Levies amongst the Sarhadis. I could guarantee that their pay would be good, and, as they were already such good fight-

THE DURBAR AT KHWASH.
Khan Bahadur (Sarhad Dar) standing.

RAIDER CHIEFS AT THE DURBAR AT KHWASH.

ing men, their training light. I also promised that many of their officers should be selected from amongst themselves.

After a short consultation they pretended to fall in with the idea, and several of the tribesmen actually enlisted then and there.

But Halil Khan got up and begged me to excuse him. He said it was not that he was not willing to serve in any corps I might wish to raise, but that he was very anxious about his wife and family, who were wandering about in the Morpeish hills. He was most eager to find them, and would look on it as an act of grace if I would permit him to go. As the whole scheme in view was to make their enlistment voluntary, I had, of course, to consent.

But he was not to go without a warning, and as he got up to leave I called him back, and looked him straight between the eyes. " Halil Khan," I said, with all the severity I could muster, " if you play me false, or ever raise your hand against me again, I will blow your head off."

He looked back at me as steadily. " Sahib, your kindness overwhelms me. I swear by the Koran " (drawing one from under his robes) " that I will never fight against you again."

" Well, I will accept your word this second time. But if you fail to keep it—remember."

And so he left, under safe conduct, and shortly afterwards Jiand, but not until I had reminded him that I had not yet received the loot he had taken, and which he, at our last meeting, had engaged to hand over. I demanded its immediate return, and laid special stress on the four tyres included in it. I also told him that he must return, at the same time, all Government camels seized when he had raided the British lines of communication, and also the four hundred Afghan camels which I had just heard his men had seized on the caravan route from Nushki to Robat.

Jiand faithfully promised that all should be returned within a couple of days of his departure from the neighbourhood of Khwash. This promise he kept to the letter, for the camels and loot arrived on the date specified.

As may be imagined, the tyres were specially welcome. Those on the car were absolutely worn out, and, of course, we had no possible means of obtaining others.

For the moment, everything seemed peaceful. So peaceful that we settled down in Khwash for a few quiet weeks; but, in the interval, did our utmost to make the place secure against all attacks.

CHAPTER IX

TREACHERY AND ITS SEQUEL

Further reinforcements—Entrenchments and gardens—Government inquiries—Food supplies—An offer to Jiand—Murad and straw—Shah Sawar again—Sentence—Idu's suggestion—Re-enter the Rose Lady—News of Jiand's intentions—A vital moment—A round-up—The Sarhad-dar's advice—A Bhusa hunt—Distrustful wives.

DURING this rest in Khwash I was able to increase to some extent the forces under my command. I obtained a whole squadron of the 28th Light Cavalry, under Colonel Claridge, and two machine guns from Nasaratabad. In addition I obtained from Kacha a considerable quantity of gun-cotton, with fuses, etc., and a supply of barbed wire, of which, fortunately, there were large stores at Kacha.

The men were kept busy with their musketry training, and with the improvements that were being made in and about the fort. We also succeeded in creating a really creditable, and very useful, garden outside the walls, with the help of a native gardener, whom I had sent for from Kacha. He brought large quantities of seeds with him, and it was amazing how, in so short a time, we were able to obtain full-grown marrows, cucumbers, pumpkins, Indian corn, turnips, carrots, lettuces and spinach. These fresh vegetables formed an invaluable addition to, and variation of, a very monotonous diet. We also sowed a considerable amount of barley of a kind which comes to maturity and ripens within three months.

The men were immensely interested in their garden, but were still more eager to toil on the serious work of improving our defences, and in the building of barracks to obtain shelter from the sun.

The forces at my disposal were, at best, infinitesimal compared with those the Raiders could collect, though, of course, the latter were at the great disadvantage of being minus mountain or machine guns. But supposing—as might happen at any moment—it became necessary to divide my forces, part to go on any expedition, and part to remain in defence of Khwash, the Raiders, if they chose to attack in numbers, could, without question, recapture their capital.

I decided, therefore, to blow up the surrounding walls of the fort, as well as the three smaller tourelles, leaving the tallest tower alone standing. In places of these raised tourelles I made an entrenched camp outside the site of the old walls. Peculiar folds in the ground lent themselves well to my purpose, enabling me to place the defensive lines along the tops of the folds. The interior of the work was thus well concealed from view.

The high tourelle was then improved and

strengthened, and a machine gun placed on its top to command the whole of the camp below.

Those Raiders dwelling in the surrounding districts took a keen interest in these changes, for they were under the impression that we had only demolished the existing walls with the intention of building stronger and higher ones, and asked me how high I intended to make them.

As I did not think it wise to gratify their curiosity, I replied that, when finished, it might be just possible to see the tops of them! From this reply the rumour got abroad that I was making a vast fortress, and, later on, the Persian Government sent urgent inquiries as to why I had built a great fort in Persia without its permission. It was, in consequence, difficult to persuade them that I had built nothing, but, on the contrary, had blown up existing walls, and that all that I had done in excess of this was to dig into the ground!

Although time was passing peacefully and busily in the organisation of these various works, I was beginning to get very anxious about the food supply of both men and beasts.

It was now the end of May and the heat was intense. The camels used in the caravans bringing supplies from India found little or no grazing between marches, and died in their dozens on the way, the consequence being that but little of the supplies despatched from India ever reached us.

Our horses began to die off in alarming numbers.

The grass on the slopes of the hills surrounding Khwash was of course quickly eaten up, and we were reduced practically to nothing, not possessing even straw as fodder. To make matters worse there were still three months to wait before we could hope to obtain straw from the barley we had sown. Altogether the position was beginning to be of an alarming nature, and I began to wonder whether, though Jiand and all his men had not been able to turn us out of Khwash, we might not be driven out by slow starvation.

Something had to be done and done quickly. No stone must be left unturned to save us from this pass, and I cast about for means of feeding the animals other than by these failing supplies from India. It was then that I suddenly remembered Jiand's crops at Kamalabad. When, on the first occasion, he had surrendered there I had spared not only the lives of himself and his followers but his crops as well. Those crops I decided to call upon him to share with us now.

Accordingly, in the early part of June, I sent for him, and in a few days he obeyed the summons, but was obviously reluctant, and very morose.

I thereupon frankly told him the position with regard to the animals, and said that I knew he must have vast quantities of bhusa from his crops, for the bulk of which he could have no use, and asked him to sell it.

The old villain refused point blank. I swallowed

my anger as best I could, and told him I would give four times the market price for it if he would send it at once.

But he was obstinate, and persisted in his refusal, in spite of all my offers.

As a matter of fact I had been told repeatedly that it was Jiand's one hope and ambition that I would try conclusions with him in his own part of the country, where his secret hiding places, and defences amidst the difficult hill country, were only known to his own tribe. Moreover, so I was also told, Halil Khan was continually urging him to force me to fight. Halil Khan himself was itching to wipe out the humiliation and discredit they had both suffered as an outcome of being bluffed twice when they could actually have wiped us out.

Indignant as I was there was nothing to be done but to let him go. I had promised him safe conduct to and fro; I, therefore, had no alternative.

But there was still another stone that could be turned. About five miles distant from the valley of Kamalabad, Jiand's stronghold, lay another fertile valley, Karsimabad, the property of an old Chief named Murad. This old man had at one time been the leader of the Sarhad, until Jiand had deposed him from his leadership and assumed it himself. Although Murad was outwardly on friendly terms with Jiand—he was not strong enough to show himself otherwise—I had heard many hints of the old ex-Chief's jealousy of and resentment towards Jiand.

I, therefore, sent for Murad and asked him if he would sell his straw, telling him that Jiand had refused to do business with me. The old fellow assured me I could have all the straw I wanted, and that I could have it for nothing. Of course I refused his generosity, told him I would pay him what I had offered Jiand, and instructed him to get it ready as soon as possible, when I would send my camels to bring it in.

Before Murad, who was obviously delighted with such a good piece of business, departed he gave me a word of warning which fully confirmed all I had heard of Halil Khan's and Jiand's smouldering enmity.

" If they can kill you, Sahib, they will. And they will most surely fight against you and try to kill you before many weeks are past."

It was about this date that repeated confirmations reached me of Shah Sawar's persistent treachery. Up to the present I had elected to ignore the incident of his letters to the Germans. They had never reached their destinations, so no harm had been done so far. It had been my constant wish, despite all the warnings I had received, to make friends with the Yarmahommedzais. But it was now time, I considered, to take some notice of Shah Sawar's activities, and this seemed a suitable moment to charge him bluntly concerning his traffic with the Germans.

Accordingly he was summoned to appear before

a drum-head court martial consisting of myself and two other officers, to be tried for repeated acts of treachery, and particularly for communication with the Germans, coupled with the information supplied to the same quarter that I had few troops, and that, if they (the Germans) came to the Sarhad it would be easy for them, with his help, to overwhelm my whole force.

As usual, Shah Sawar swore he was innocent of all these charges and pointed out that it was obvious he could not possibly have been guilty, as he could not write.

Then I played a trump card, for I produced the mullah (priest) who had written the letters at his dictation, and who had wandered, a day or so before, into the camp.

When Shah Sawar caught sight of the mullah he shrugged his shoulders and muttered, "Kismet." He knew the game was up, confessed at once that he had dictated the letters, and had put his mark to them.

There was naturally only one sentence that could be passed upon him, and he knew it. He was found guilty and condemned to be shot. He implored me to give him another chance, but I was tired of his broken promises, and told him flatly that he had offended once too often. He had been convicted by a duly constituted court martial, and the finding of the court must stand. I told him also that his time was short, and advised him to write any farewell messages he wanted to send, and to make his will as quickly as possible. The mullah was also given leave to write anything that Shah Sawar wished to dictate.

As I passed from the tent I gazed hard at Shah Sawar. The sweat was pouring down his face—few men can hear the sentence of immediate death without emotion of some sort—but he did not utter a sound. It must be admitted that he bore himself like a man, as, with a gesture of resignation, he told the mullah he wanted him to start writing at once.

Whilst he was writing out his last wishes, I made my way to the Durbar tent to wait until he had finished. On my way I met Idu and told him the result of the court martial. Idu had an uncanny gift of intuition and I am certain realised how much I disliked my obvious but uncongenial duty. He looked at me strangely and then disappeared.

Some little time later I was leaving the tent when I caught sight of the Gul-Bibi, Shah Sawar's wife, dressed in her very best attire, running towards me. Directly she reached me, she fell on her knees and, touching my feet with her hands, broke into lamentations.

"What is it?" I asked, trying to speak sternly. "What have you to say?"

The Gul-Bibi had a great deal to say! She said that Idu had gone to her and told her of the sentence that had been passed on her husband and she had come to plead for his life. She used every argument she could think of to persuade me to reverse the finding of the court, and finally went bail in her own person for the future good behaviour of the handsome rascal, if only he might have another chance.

" I swear to you," she said passionately, " that if ever my fool of a husband raises his hand against you again or breaks his word to you, I will shoot him with my own hands. I, the Gul-Bibi, swear it."

It occurred to me that after all it might be politic to temper justice with mercy. Shah Sawar undoubtedly had great influence and the concession of his life might be a turning-point in the determination of his tribe to be loyal to the British cause.

I said that she had accomplished what no one else could have done and that her eloquence had persuaded me to grant her her husband's life.

" But this is the very last time I will show him any mercy. Shah Sawar has proved himself a traitor and has broken his oath again and again. I am only letting him go now on your guarantee of his good behaviour in the future. If ever he breaks faith again, it will be for the very last time. You may go now and tell him what I have said and tell him that he owes his life entirely to you."

I directed her to the tent where she would find Shah Sawar waiting for death, and presently she returned with her husband by her side. He was obviously very subdued and very impressed. His gratitude was genuine enough, anyhow for the moment, and once more he promised that he would never fight again—etc., etc.

The next day a message was received from Murad to the effect that he had collected a fine quantity of bhusa, and that it was piled up in fourteen great stacks ready for transport, if camels could be sent to fetch it.

Word was sent back that I would go myself on the morrow to Karsimabad with the camels, and a small escort, in order that it might be possible to thank and pay him in person.

Accordingly orders were given for the escort and camels to be ready to start early the next morning.

But, that night, news was brought by one of Landon's intelligence men which caused a modification of these plans.

It should here be mentioned that Major Landon had, shortly before, been obliged to leave me. It will be remembered that he was one of but three Intelligence Officers in Persia, and had therefore to return to his duties. His place as my Brigade Major had been taken by a very able Staff Officer, Major Sanders of the 36th Sikhs.

The news the scout brought me was to the effect that Jiand knew all about my proposed visit to Karsimabad, and was planning to attack in force, and capture me. He had been waiting for a good opportunity to lure me out of Khwash, and now felt he had his chance.

"Well, he shall have it," I replied. "Only, we

will disappoint him. For instead of going with only a small escort, we'll take a good part of our entire army, and the guns. He'll then have his work cut out."

The consequence being that when we marched out on the following morning we made an imposing spectacle. I determined to do the thing thoroughly, so took a considerable number of infantry, the cavalry, guns and a large convoy of camels.

We had only marched a short distance when one of the scouts came in with the information that all the bhusa at Karsimabad had been burned.

At first I could hardly believe my ears and told him he must be mistaken; that perhaps some of it had been burned by accident, but that fourteen stacks, the number Murad had mentioned as collected, could not all have been burned by this means. But the man proceeded to tell me that it was no accident. He himself had seen the scorched ground upon which the stacks had stood. They had been built sufficiently far apart to make it impossible to be burned by one setting light to another. Each stack had been separately and individually fired, and Murad had proof that it had been done by Jiand's men.

As may be imagined, I was nearly beside myself with rage at the news. It would entail untold suffering amongst our unfortunate beasts, who were already underfed. The act was unforgivable, especially when we were just hoping to obtain a safeguard against the worst months of the year.

The march of the column was immediately quickened. There remained but one thing to do—to go forward and ascertain the truth. If Jiand had really been guilty of this act he should be accommodated as regards fighting. So far everything possible had been done to create friendly relations with him, and over and above this he had been, throughout, generously and leniently treated. But patience has its limits, and there could be no more leniency.

Despite the burning heat we managed to cover the distance in record time, and were within five miles of Karsimabad when the advance guard reported the enemy in sight, and in large numbers.

"Come out to capture me, I suppose!" I remarked to Sanders. "Jiand is, probably, still under the impression that we are coming with only a small escort. I wonder what he'll do when he sees the column—and the guns?"

What he did do we were soon to know. The old villain must have indulged in one short look to realise, once again, that he had been foiled in his attempt at a surprise; for I knew, by current rumour, that he stood in deadly terror of what the guns could do. He had certainly never seen them working, but had heard the rattle of the Maxims at Koh-i-taftan, and had a wholesome dread of their destructive possibilities. When, therefore, the cavalry and the guns came into view, instead of attacking, he sent

IN DIFFICULTIES BETWEEN NASARATABAD AND ROBAT.

a messenger ahead to meet me, and to ask whether he might come and do me honour!

"Tell him," I replied, still furiously angry, "that it is not a case of may he come—he must come himself and instantly. I am in no playful mood as he will find to his cost."

A few minutes later we saw Jiand, accompanied by two or three men ambling towards us on his camel. Immediately on his arrival Jiand assured me that, hearing I was in the neighbourhood, he had come with his followers to do me honour.

"Honour be damned!" I retorted. "What do you mean by burning the bhusa I have bought from Murad? Was that also by way of doing me honour?"

Jiand protested his innocence. Was it possible that anything that belonged to the General Sahib should, or could, be burned? And how could he (the General) so wrong him (Jiand) as to suspect him of any such offence? If the bhusa really was burned, he swore that he was innocent, and had had nothing to do with it.

"We'll soon prove whether you had or not," I returned. "I am on my way to Karsimabad to inquire into it. You will go there too, and if I find you had a hand in it, as I am convinced you had, you shall regret it to your dying day. Go on in front of me, and wait for me in Karsimabad."

With a sullen face Jiand obeyed, and our own force continued its march.

Arrived within three-quarters of a mile of Murad's place we halted at what appeared to be a favourable place to camp. This represented a hard flat piece of ground at the base of a small hill. A picket on the hill-top would command the surrounding country and so prevent surprise.

The bulk of the force was left and I went forward with an escort of about a dozen infantrymen and some fifteen cavalrymen.

At the entrance to Karsimabad I noticed a huge tree with a mud platform placed round its base, close beside the ruins of a small fort. This seemed to offer an ideal spot upon which to hold the inquiry, for the tree afforded a wide circle of shade from the burning heat.

Accordingly I sat down, with Sanders and the Sarhad-dar on either side, whilst the cavalry accompanying us dismounted and remained behind the tree. The infantry-escort formed up on our right.

Murad, who appeared greatly distressed, came forward and told me that all the bhusa he had collected for us had been burned down, thus confirming the report I had already received.

"Who did it?" I thundered. "Can you produce the man who dared to burn my property?"

To my great surprise Murad said he could. He had captured the man, a Yarmahommedzai.

Scarcely had the man been brought forward when, from every quarter, appeared men armed with rifles. A moment before the place, excepting for ourselves, had been empty. These men seemed to have sprung out of the ground, but must, actually, have been concealed in the adjoining fields. In an instant I could tell that they were picked men of Jiand's lashkar. There must have been between one hundred and fifty and two hundred of them. They came forward and squatted down in a circle close in front of us; Jiand, and his kinsman and evil genius, a man named Nur-Mahommed, placing themselves well in the foreground.

In a flash I realised the tactical error I had made in leaving the main force three-quarters of a mile away, and before I had made certain that Jiand's men had not occupied Karsimabad. These men held their magazine rifles, which were always loaded, across their knees. From where we sat, I now realised, and too late, that I could not see, or signal to, my own small force, and that, except by a miracle, it would be equally ignorant of these proceedings. I glanced quickly behind me at the fifteen or sixteen cavalrymen I had brought, saw that they had dismounted and were holding their lances in their hands, whilst their rifles remained in the buckets on the off-sides of the horses. A bad position for getting at them when dismounted and at a moment's notice.

It was obvious that I had allowed myself to be caught in a trap. We all knew it, though not one man with me showed it by the quiver of an eyelid.

I turned to the man whom Murad had brought

forward and placed before me as the burner of the stacks of straw.

" How dare you burn my bhusa? What reason had you for doing it, and who told you to do it? "

Before the man, who was trembling like a leaf, had time to answer, Nur-Mahommed sprang up and shouted:

" The country is ours and everything in it. We will burn the bhusa, or burn anything we like."

And he glared at Sanders and myself in a way that left no doubt as to his meaning.

I told him angrily to sit down, as I was not talking to him. For answer he assumed a threatening attitude, and openly sneered at me for attempting to give orders I could not enforce.

I ordered a sepoy to arrest him.

What followed all happened in a flash.

The sepoy had scarcely moved a step to obey when every one of Jiand's men leapt to their feet and brought their rifles to the present.

I must confess to having acted automatically. Indeed, there was no time to think or do otherwise.

I literally roared at them. " How dare you, you dogs? Sit down this instant! "

I reached out my hands towards Jiand who was close to me, and, in a paroxysm of rage, forced him down by my side.

" Sit down! " I roared again into the dark faces of the men surrounding us.

Hesitation and doubt spread amongst that

threatening crowd—and the bulk of them sat down!

They were now given no time to recover their poise. Sanders and the escort were at once ordered to disarm the men who remained standing.

Like a flash my men darted forward, only too thankful to take action instead of waiting to be shot down, and in a twinkling had wrenched their rifles from the scowling brutes who were hesitating as to whether they would shoot first or submit. They were looking to their Chief for a lead. But Jiand, that once invincible warrior, had lost his nerve, and now sat cowering, unable either to make a decision or dominate his own men.

So, whilst they stood, furtive and undecided, they were disarmed and left helpless.

" Now," I shouted, turning to those who had sat down, " get up and place your rifles against that wall, there," pointing to the wall of the mud fort. " And if there is the slightest sign of treachery I will shoot you down like the dogs you are."

Like a lot of beaten sheep they got up and obeyed.

The danger was over before we had had time fully to realise it.

I then proceeded to tell the Raiders what I thought of them in language which has since been reported as hectic. They were told that their lives and their property had been spared again and again; that over and over again their liberty had been given them when they should have been kept as prisoners. But this time their offence was beyond forgiveness and they should now have a taste of the treatment they deserved.

I then ordered my escort to seize and tie the men together, and drive them back to the camp. A certain number of the Yarmahommedzais leapt up at this, and, before they could be stopped, had bolted into the high-grown crops surrounding the place. But we caught a good sixty of them, and these were bound by their hands in groups of three by their turbans. They were then marched off to the main column, which had remained in blissful ignorance of these happenings a short three-quarters of a mile away.

Sanders and I remained where we were, and a few minutes later the Sarhad-dar returned, wiping the sweat from his face.

"That was a close shave, Sahib," he said, and I could see that his hands were shaking, despite the fact that he had behaved with the utmost bravery during the crisis. "Though so many got away, amongst those we have captured are nearly all the leading men of the Yarmahommedzais. Without them the tribe will be as men without leaders, and we need not fear them. I have searched and questioned some of them, and I have indisputable proofs that they came to capture you. They wanted you—alive, not dead, that they might be able to dictate their own terms."

"Well," I said disgustedly, "I've had enough in the way of trying to make friends with them. I know that both you and Idu have advised all along that it would be of no use, but I have hoped against hope. Now the Indian Government must deal with them, and I shall advise the Government that the best thing to do will be to send them to India and imprison them there."

The Sarhad-dar replied, with heartfelt relief, "I am thankful you have at last come to that decision. It's the only chance of obtaining peace in the Sarhad. Juma Khan has already given ample proof of his loyalty, and Halil Khan, untrustworthy as he is, would never dream of fighting the Sirkar alone. If I may advise I would suggest that whoever is ultimately set free Nur-Mahommed is never liberated. He is Jiand's evil genius. Without him you might have won over Jiand to real loyalty, but so long as Nur-Mahommed, who is a devil, is always whispering in his ear you can never trust Jiand to keep any oath."

Before we left Karsimabad I paid Murad some compensation for his straw, for he had had the best intentions.

When we reached the main column, which was now agog with curiosity, I once again combed out our prisoners, retaining some forty-three and letting the others go. It must be remembered that we were desperately short of food ourselves and I did not want a single unnecessary mouth to feed.

But I was not going back to Khwash without a supply of fodder for our animals. I, therefore, told Jiand that as he had burned the bhusa I had bought, and had refused his own at the generous price offered, I should now take his without payment.

So we made a détour by way of Kamalabad, where my men immediately started hunting for straw and wheat. We eventually found that the latter had been carefully hidden by Jiand, and in a highly ingenious way. The wheat had been put into sacks, and buried in the sand dunes. The sand had then been carefully smoothed over, leaving nothing to show that it had been disturbed.

But, before our search, I asked the Sarhad-dar, " How on earth will the men find the sacks? " fearful lest, after all, Jiand had foiled me.

" They know how to find it," he replied. " Give them the order to search for it and you'll see what they'll do. They know the trick well enough."

Accordingly, orders were issued to search for, and carry off, all the sacks of wheat and all bhusa that could be found.

In an instant they were at work amongst the sand dunes, prodding in the sand with their cleaning rods. Every now and again a man would shout " Here! " and after a few minutes' digging a sack would be dragged to light.

It was immensely interesting to watch this unearthing of plunder, and after a while I called " Give me a cleaning rod and let me try."

But I proved a hopeless exponent of the game. Prod as I would, I could find nothing, though the smiling Rekis would prod where I had drawn blank and fish out several sacks. This wheat was a great find, and was loaded on to the camels with the greatest care.

From Kamalabad I sent a couple of men ahead with messages to Colonel Claridge—who had remained behind in charge of Khwash—telling him briefly what had happened, and asking him to prepare a barbed wire cage for the prisoners now being brought in.

So promptly did he set to work that, when we marched in next day, there was ready as perfect a cage as any commander could wish to have.

We were given a great reception by the garrison, delighted at the plunder we had brought. The bhusa meant the saving of our animals, and the wheat was invaluable to ourselves, as our supply of flour had begun to run very short.

The wheat was given to the ladies of Khwash to grind outside the camp. These industrious females all possessed little stone hand-mills, and, for many days afterwards, the air was filled with the sound of these at work. These same ladies implored me to pay them in person for their work, because, they informed me, their men-folk were not to be trusted. It appeared on inquiry that when the men were paid they were apt to put the wages of their wives' labour into their own pockets. So, each afternoon, for some days, we had a pay-parade of Khwashi ladies to receive in rupees the wages they had honestly earned.

While I was waiting for Government instructions as to the disposal of our Yarmahommedzai prisoners I made these work at strengthening the camp. It was not easy to get much work out of them as they strongly resented being put to what they considered to be a degradation. They maintained it to be a gross indignity for a fighting man to be made to work with his hands, and contended that all manual labour should be performed by lower caste people such as the Khwashis.

But honest work did not hurt them, for, during their imprisonment, their health improved to a remarkable extent. This result was probably due to the increased variety of their rations, and to the vegetables grown in our new garden which they shared with the garrison.

CHAPTER X

FAILURE AND FRESH PLANS

Slave buying—A diet discovery—Poetic justice—Disposition of prisoners—Incredible news—The Sawar's story—Disposal of forces—The march to Kamalabad—Jiand gains his freedom—Retreat to Khwash.

WHILST waiting instructions from the Indian Government as to the disposal of our Sarhadi prisoners I turned my attention to the slave question. This had long been one of my pre-occupations. The chief trouble lay in the fact that not only the Yarmahommedzais and the Gamshadzais, but also the friendly Rekis—the men of Idu's tribe—possessed large numbers of these unfortunate women and children. The consequence was that, when I announced that an order was about to be issued commanding the surrender of all slaves throughout the Sarhad, Idu openly groused.

He pointed out that it would be a great hardship on his fellow-tribesmen. Many of them had not actually engaged in raids, but had honourably bought, and paid for, the women from their captors, and that, in consequence, they would not only be out of pocket to the extent of the purchase price but would, also, be without servants to do their menial work.

Idu's point of view was clear enough, but he was asked, " what about the unfortunate slaves? "

The Sarhad-dar backed me up for all he was worth, and at last a compromise was made. The order went forth that the slaves must all be liberated without question, but that, as the Rekis had aided us in every possible way, the Government would purchase their slaves at the rate of three hundred rupees for a woman, seventy-five for a girl, and twenty-five for a boy.

In due course slaves began to arrive from every direction, though undoubtedly the order was ignored in every instance where it was possible to do so. At last, in order to accelerate delivery, it was necessary to promise to purchase all slaves, no matter by whom owned. From that moment it was astonishing how the number increased, some arriving on camels, others on foot. The condition of these wretched women and children was pitiable in the extreme. Some of them were those whom Izzat had captured during his recent big raid, but the majority had been in captivity for many years and were in a wretched state, half-starved, half-naked, and cowed, as the outcome of evident ill-treatment. Many appeared to have lost all hope in life.

These poor folk were given quarters amongst the Khwashis, special *jugis* being set aside for them, and were gradually restored to some semblance of civilised humanity. White army drill and brightly coloured prints, were requisitioned from Kacha.

RAIDED SLAVES ON THE WAY TO THEIR HOMES.

A PERSIAN GIRL CAPTURED BY JUMA KHAN, AND WHO ESCAPED TO KHWASH.

With these materials the Khwashi ladies made garments for our enfranchised slaves. It was pitiful to see their joy and gratitude when told that they were now free, and would shortly be sent back to their own homes.

One of our new guests became a constant source of wonder to us all. She was a fine, well-grown, attractive young woman of about nineteen or twenty, and had been a captive in the hands of a Gamshadzai Chief. When she heard of the order that all slaves were to be released she claimed her freedom, and her right to go to the British General at Khwash, where safe asylum was offered to all Persian slaves. Her Gamshadzai master, however, had not the slightest intention of letting her go. She was far too useful.

But this Persian girl possessed both grit and powers of endurance. One night she escaped in the darkness, and, though pursued for a long distance by her captor, managed to elude him, and made good her escape. Apparently she ran all through the night, covering fully forty miles over rough precipitous hills and sandy plains. It seemed an incredible feat—at first none of us believed the tale—but she provided such striking evidence of it that we had at last to believe her.

Poor soul, she was very dirty, her feet were bare and her clothing torn to ribbons, but in her pride and joy at being free once more, she was a moving picture.

The emaciated condition of these slaves filled us all with commiseration, and when it was commented upon amongst ourselves the Sarhad-dar remarked grimly, " You can't have seen their staple food. If you had, you wouldn't wonder. They carry it in those little bags they all bring in with them."

My curiosity was aroused and I asked some of the women to show me what was contained in those bags. They promptly told me that they contained the only food they were allowed by their captors, apart from any green stuff they were themselves able to gather wild on the hillsides. Some of the bags were then emptied, and quantities of dried beetles were poured out on the ground.

Incredible as it seems close inquiry confirmed their statement—that these dried beetles formed the greater part of their diet. With this evidence one could no longer wonder that these poor creatures were in such a wretched, cowed and hopeless state.

When as many slaves were collected as could be accommodated it became needful to send them off in order to make room for others, and also to obviate the necessity of feeding them. Moreover, now that this batch had begun to regain its humanity, its members were very anxious to return to their own homes, and when it was announced that we were going to repatriate them under escort they fell to laughing and crying with joy. When they were told that this would be done under the charge of Izzat—

the Yarmahommedzai who had captured so many of them—their joy was turned to dismay, and they implored me not to trust them to his tender mercies, but to send them with anyone else, for he would surely take them back again into captivity.

"I have decided on Izzat," I replied, "because he is a Chief who has plenty of camels of his own for your transport, and, as he stole so many of you, he will know exactly where to return you. But you shall hear yourselves what I am going to say to him. If, then, you are not satisfied, I will choose someone else. You shall decide for yourselves."

Accordingly Izzat was sent for, and informed of this order. I considered it a piece of poetic justice that he should be the one to restore the people whom he had stolen, and whose lives he had ruined. Izzat listened grimly and I fancied I could detect in his dark eyes a hint of what he proposed doing when these women were once again in his power.

"And," I added quietly, "you will bring back and place in my hands a letter from every one of the women I put in your care. I have the names of all of them written down. These letters must be written individually by each woman after she has safely reached her own home, and must also state that she has been well used on the way. If there is lacking a letter from any single one of these women, when you return to Khwash, I shall hang every member of your family on the tree under which I am now sitting, and you will then be able to count their dead bodies for yourself. They will remain in my charge during your absence."

Izzat could see that I meant what I said. " Sahib, I am in your hands. I will do whatever you say."

I then turned to the eager Persian women.

" You have heard what has been said. You have listened to the conditions made, and which Izzat has accepted. Are you willing now to go with him? "

They all assured me they were, and a day or so later the cavalcade set out, Izzat taking sufficient camels to allow for the accommodation of all who were infirm and weak, and for the fitter members to be able to ride turn and turn about, also for the portage of sufficient food for their long trek of some one hundred and fifty miles into the Narmashir.

As may be imagined it was a great relief to us all when we had seen them safely on their way. I should here record the fact that, in due course, Izzat returned, bearing letters from every one of the slaves to the effect that they had safely arrived at their own homes. He dared not risk the penalty he knew would have surely been exacted had he failed in his trust.

After some little delay I received from Quetta an answer to my request for instructions as to the disposal of the Sarhadi prisoners. This answer directed that they should be sent straight to Quetta, a distance of something like four hundred and fifty miles.

Naturally I had not sufficient troops to spare for an adequate escort on such a long march, and sent an answer to that effect; but, at the same time, suggested that if the Government could arrange for escort, by Indian troops from Saindak (about nine marches from Khwash), I could arrange to police them that distance.

After waiting another two weeks, word came that three hundred of the 106th Hazara Pioneers would be sent to Saindak to take them over, and I was requested to send the prisoners there, under escort, without delay. I was also informed that a wireless troop was immediately being dispatched to Khwash, the purpose being to open up easier communication with India. At this period the only method of such communication was by wire from Robat, or Kacha, to Quetta, and camel messengers had then to be employed to take messages from Robat, or Kacha, to Khwash, a not always reliable, and often lengthy, proceeding.

Accordingly, when I knew the exact date of the Hazaras' arrival at Saindak, I made my own dispositions for sending the Sarhadi prisoners there. It should be clearly understood that the whole of the rough, roadless district lying between these two places was over-run by the enemy, and, moreover, an enemy deeply resentful of the fact that so many of their Chiefs were in our hands. It must be remembered, too, that our numbers were, compared with theirs, ludicrously small.

We calculated, however, and reasonably I think, on the unlikelihood of an attack by the Yarmahommedzais on the column, owing to the presence of the more important prisoners, whose lives they would not dare to endanger. It was, therefore, thought absolutely safe for the wireless troop, who would be accompanied by a small escort only, to come through to us at the same time as, and on a parallel route to, that of the prisoners, though the two parties were marching in opposite directions. The wireless troop had orders to come South along the Eastern slopes of the Koh-i-taftan, and the prisoners were to be marched North over the Western slopes of the same peak.

I decided also to send as large an escort as possible with the prisoners, my object being to ensure against any contretemps prior to their receipt by the Hazaras —a magnificent type of fighting man—for conduct to India. I also had another reason, for I had been warned, by repeated rumour, that Halil Khan was then occupied in gathering his entire forces together for the rescue of Jiand and his men whilst being marched northward to Saindak.

Our own garrison was, therefore, practically reduced to a skeleton, whilst a force consisting of three troops of cavalry, seventy-five infantry(about three-fourths of our total numbers) and two maxims, under the command of two white officers, was detached for escort duties.

This column started early one morning in July, and was to march eighteen miles on the first day.

That same night, or rather early on the following

CAPTURED RAIDERS ON THE WAY TO KACHHA.

morning, for it was about two a.m., I was awakened in my tent and informed that a sawar had just arrived with an urgent message for me. A moment later one of the cavalrymen composing the escort, which had started so gaily about twenty hours before, came in, breathing quickly and heavily with the speed at which he had ridden. He told me that he had ridden as he had never ridden before to bring me a message from the officer commanding the prisoners' escort. It was to the effect that every one of the prisoners, save Jiand and one of his sons, had escaped in the darkness, and that he awaited further orders in the circumstances.

For a moment I thought I was still asleep and dreaming. How could it be possible that forty-five unarmed men had succeeded in escaping from an armed, and numerically larger, escort?

But the stark truth was at last forced upon me, and it amounted to nothing short of absolute disaster. The whole of my four months' work had been undone in a few hours, and I was confronted with the knowledge that I should now have to make a humiliating confession of utter failure, and at the very moment when the work I had been sent to do seemed so nearly and successfully finished.

The situation resolved itself into this; not only would it now be impossible to hand over our enemy and ringleaders to the large armed escort now on its way, and especially detailed to receive them, but these escaped Chiefs would be able to reorganise and hearten up their people, who had remained quiet during the past few weeks simply because they had been without their leadership.

These same Chiefs, of course, knew to a man the strength of our force, and were naturally bitter with resentment as an outcome of their recent captivity. They would, I knew, now leave no stone unturned in their endeavour to wipe us out. My feelings can be better imagined than described.

The Sawar was questioned closely as to this disastrous affair, and I obtained the following details.

The escort had pitched its camp before sundown on an open hillside. An enclosure, or sort of rough zareba, had been constructed with a few strands of barbed wire, and the prisoners, with the exception of Jiand and his son, had been placed inside, and sentries set over them. Jiand and his son had been kept apart, in a small *jugi*, with a sentry in front of it.

It was a very dark, quiet night, and the camp had soon settled down to sleep.

Suddenly, strange stealthy sounds had been heard close to the zareba, and the sentries had fired wildly into the darkness. Instantly the whole camp had been roused, and the officers had rushed to the prisoners' quarters.

Lamps were brought, and it was quickly found that the zareba was empty. What had happened seemed fairly obvious. The prisoners had evidently taken off all their clothes and flung the heavier garments over the barbed wire. This done, and acting in consort, they had broken or borne it down by sheer weight. In any case the whole lot of them had escaped, absolutely naked, leaving their clothes behind on the barbed wire!

Of course an immediate search was instituted, but the Raiders had escaped into the rough, broken hills during the few minutes succeeding the alarm, and not a single one was re-taken. The only prisoners now left in our hands were Jiand and his son.

After such a set-back a man may be pardoned for being at his wits' end. Not only did it spell failure to keep faith with the Indian Government in regard to the prisoners, but it became plain that the wireless troop, whose safe passage I had practically guaranteed, was now in peril; for they would, almost certainly, be attacked, as they must by this time be right in the heart of the enemy territory, whose fighting men would now be elated beyond bounds at their successful coup.

I quickly realised that we must act without an instant's delay. We must first rescue that wireless troop with its small escort at any cost. The best thing to be done at the moment was to order the prisoners' escort—who now had no one to escort! except Jiand and his son—to proceed instantly in the direction along which the wireless troop was coming, whilst Sanders and myself, with every man we could collect after leaving some sort of garrison for Khwash —goodness knows we were few enough already!—

set out to join up with the escort, which would have to march due East that day.

I could then take some of the men forming that escort and go in the direction of Kamalabad with the object of holding off the Gamshadzais under Halil Khan; I was convinced they would now, without question, put into execution the threat they had so repeatedly made of trying to rescue Jiand. As will be seen my objective was the Kamalabad valley, where I should at least have a better chance of holding them up than elsewhere.

The messenger was thereupon directed to return at once to the officer commanding the escort, with a letter directing the new move and telling him at what point I would intersect his march that evening.

As soon as he had been dispatched a servant was sent to awaken Sanders, Idu and the Sarhad-dar, and summon them immediately to my tent. When they were told the bad news their dismay was fully equal to mine. The Sarhad-dar seemed to think the world had come to an end. The situation was in any case quite black enough, and it was a very depressed little party that an hour later set out from the camp.

It was not until well on into the evening that the force composing the prisoners' escort joined us at the appointed *rendezvous*, but when it did I proceeded to re-arrange the composition of units without delay. I took twenty-five cavalry, some fifty of the infantry, also the two machine guns, and ordered the officer commanding, who was desperately downcast at the disaster, to march at top speed with the force left him in the direction along which the wireless troop must now be coming. His further orders, on getting in touch, were to tell them what had happened, and, as I did not now consider it safe for them to come at present to Khwash, to go back with him to Saindak, where he was to hand over Jiand and his son to the Hazaras now waiting to receive them.

He was further instructed to say that I was marching in another direction, towards Kamalabad, in an endeavour to hold up Halil Khan and the Gamshadzais, who, according to rumours reaching us that evening, were on their way in great force to Gusht, at the end of the Kamalabad valley.

My little force started then and there, marching a distance of about twelve miles through the night, and reached Kamalabad before daybreak. It must be remembered that campaigning under conditions obtaining in a district such as the Sarhad is utterly different from that of any other type of warfare.

Amongst my own little force, and especially amongst the camp followers, were both friends and potential foes, traitors and spies. In addition to this the whole population of the country was its fighting force, nearly every man being armed and trained to fight. Rumour, and news carried by runners, take the place of the dispatches and newspapers of the West, the consequence being that one's movements are conveyed from mouth to mouth immediately upon that movement taking place. This fact will in itself account for our being able to hear such constant and detailed news of both the enemy's movements and intentions—and vice versa.

No sooner had we reached Kamalabad than we learned that Halil Khan had just been there, but had taken to the Morpeish Hills as we approached. He had every intention of fighting, but wanted to do it on ground of his own choice. In any case he did not want to fight in the open, where our Maxim guns would undoubtedly have given us a great advantage.

It was a great relief to hear this, for it meant that we had intercepted him, and now stood between him and the escort with Jiand. It meant in effect that he could not attack it without first meeting and defeating us. Jiand and his son at any rate—and, after all, Jiand was the supreme Chief—would now be safely handed over at Saindak.

But my satisfaction on this point was very short lived. Soon after reaching Kamalabad another messenger, sent off post-haste by the officer in charge of the escort, arrived with the news that they had been attacked in force, and that Jiand and his son had been rescued!

I questioned the man closely as to what had happened, and discovered that Jiand and his son had been actually snatched from the very hands of their gaolers. The fight had been a long and hard one;

many men on our side had been killed, both the British officers wounded, and many rifles and much ammunition captured. It seemed that the whole force might have been annihilated but for the opportune arrival on the scene of the wireless troop with their escort. The Yarmahommedzais evidently thought this troop the advance guard of reinforcements and retired, taking Jiand and his son with them.

I learned later that the rescue party consisted of nineteen of the very men who had escaped from the prisoners' escort two nights before. It appears that they had run all the way to Kamalabad naked, had clothed and re-armed themselves, and had gone back to rescue their Chief.

One could not but admire such a magnificent feat of daring and endurance, even though it added enormously to the difficulties of our own position.

The Gamshadzais, in all probability, already knew what had happened. They would also know that I had brought only a very small detachment to Kamalabad, that merely a beaten remnant of the escort, now without British officers, was left on the slopes of the Koh-i-taftan, and that there was a still smaller force in Khwash.

It was obviously hopeless now to attempt to fight where we were. It was equally obvious that our best course would be to get back to Khwash with all speed. Khwash still remained a dominating factor, and was still in our hands. From that vantage point it might yet be possible to collect our scattered forces, and obtain reinforcements.

Flushed with victory, and elated at his escape, Jiand would also remember the importance of Khwash, and would doubtless soon be on his way thither, if, indeed, he was not already marching upon it.

So, once again, it was to be a race between us for the capital of the Sarhad.

And, as on that former occasion of a few months ago, we won the race, but our return was a very different affair to that of our previous triumphant entry.

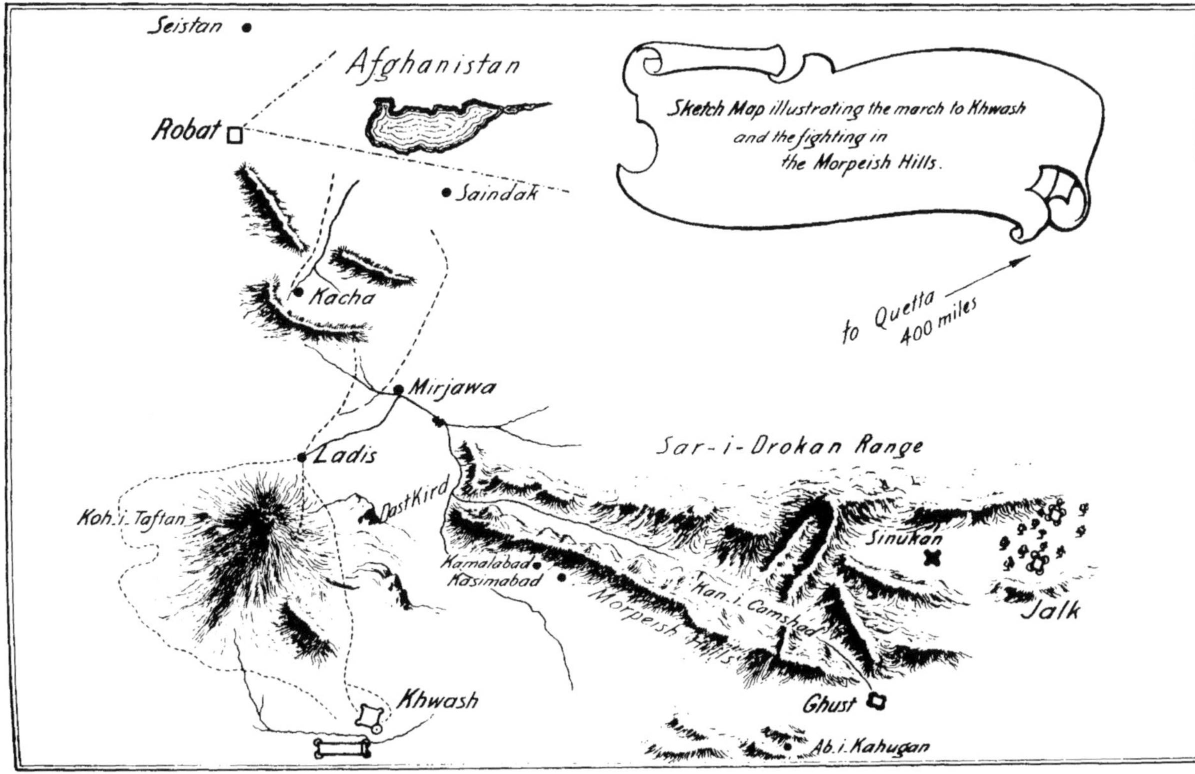
Sketch Map illustrating the march to Khwash
and the fighting in
the Morpeish Hills.
Seistan
Afghanistan
Robat
Saindak
Kacha
to Quetta
400 miles
Mirjawa
Ladis
Sar-i-Drokan Range
DastKird
Koh.i. Taftan
Kamalabad
Kasimabad
Morpeish Hills
Kan.i. Camshad
Sinukan
Jalk
Khwash
Ghust
Ab.i.Kahugan

CHAPTER XI

SUCCESS IN MINIATURE

The night attack—The Hazaras arrive—Jiand retires—We march on the Sar-i-drokan valley—Cavalry strategy—" Gushti's " decision and opinion—" The Hole of Judgment "—Attack and retirement—A lost and regained water-supply—The Sarhadis as humorists—The mud fort—Halil Khan's arrival—The fight at dawn—Exit Halil Khan—A prophet—The Hazaras' request.

IMMEDIATELY on re-entering Khwash Colonel Claridge was sent out, with all the men it was possible to spare, in an endeavour to find, and bring back, the strayed remnants of the prisoners' escort. In the meantime a camel messenger was dispatched to Saindak asking the O.C. of the Hazaras to march South to our help at once, and to take a route by which they might, with luck, join up with Colonel Claridge. A messenger was also dispatched to Colonel Dale, then commanding at Kacha, requesting him to send us all the supplies and ammunition he could spare, and personally to do his utmost to expedite the Hazaras, who were also in his immediate sphere of command.

Hardly had Colonel Claridge and his small detachment left Khwash when Jiand, with a large force, took up his position among the low hills about three miles to the North-East of the town, and Shah Sawar, who, as I might have expected, was now in full and open revolt, worried us from the hills to the South-West.

But we were not going to admit yet that we were beaten. Daily we left the camp for the open as a challenge to Jiand to come out of his hills and fight, though it must be confessed that we hoped he would not accept it.

At last, after a good deal of apparent indecision, the two Chiefs made up their minds to attack us, and by night.

I must explain that in order, as far as possible, to deceive the enemy as to our numbers—or rather lack of them—the whole of our newly entrenched camp remained occupied by day; nor did we spare any device likely to give the impression of a larger garrison. But at night the men were withdrawn to a small, strongly fortified sector of the camp, so as to consolidate our strength. One of our Maxims had been placed in this sector, the other on the only tourelle left standing, and trained on the camp.

As we were always expecting a night attack, we were thus well prepared for it when it came. Jiand made his at the North-East and Shah Sawar at the South-West angles of the camp: and when the presence of large numbers of the enemy became apparent round these areas, our men started to shoot wildly, but were quickly steadied, and ordered to hold fire. The whole of our depositions had been made with the object of allowing the enemy, if the attack came by night, actually to enter the camp, and so enable us to deal with them in denser formation.

The outer defences were rushed, and from the temporary pause that occurred it was clear that the enemy was surprised at finding no defence. This was of course the vital moment at which to let them know we were alive.

From my position in the defensive section of the camp I had had a telephone line laid to the tourelle. It was, therefore, possible to order the two Maxims to open simultaneous fire, and, at the same time, a heavy rifle fire right into the heart of those undefended sectors.

The enemy recognised that a night surprise had failed, and were evidently not inclined to continue the fight under conditions so very unfavourable to themselves, so beat a hasty retreat. The night was very dark, and so the results of our fire were not observable. Rumour said that the enemy had suffered heavily in dead and wounded, but they must have removed their casualties as there was nothing to be seen in the morning. The results were all I desired, as we were not attacked again.

Three or four days later we were much elated to learn that a junction had been effected between Colonel Claridge, the remnant of the prisoners' escort, and the three hundred men of the 106th Hazara Pioneers under Major Lang. The same information showed that they were marching together, as quickly as possible, on Khwash, and would probably be in that day. This was good news indeed.

When they did arrive my spirits rose higher still. The Hazaras were a splendid body of men, all spoiling for a fight, and I promptly arranged that they should have it. It will be remembered that the Hazaras are Shiahs, hence their eagerness to blot out as many of the Sunni Sarhadis, per man, as they could manage.

Directly Jiand became aware of their arrival he realised that it would be simply waste of time to remain in the neighbourhood of Khwash. He had now not the slightest hope of capturing it, so withdrew, with all his forces, to the Sar-i-drokan valley, which, it will be remembered, was his Summer haunt. This valley lies parallel with the Kamalabad valley, but on the farther side of the Morpeish Hills, and is bounded on its Northern side by the Sar-i-drokan Range.

It seemed now that there might be a good chance of fighting Jiand with real hope of success, and with the elimination of bluff, upon which it would no longer be of any use to rely.

Could we but defeat him in a square and open fight our past failures would be amply avenged, and British prestige again in the ascendant.

So, with this object in view, messages were sent telling him to look to himself, for we were coming, not only to fight him, but to lift all his herds. Jiand

ON THE MARCH TOWARDS 'GHUSHT AND THE MORPEISH HILLS.

replied with the defiant message that he was quite ready for us, and that he knew how to defend his herds, as well as his men, from all comers.

The Hazaras were given a couple of days' rest after their long, rapid march, and we then set out. The combined force now consisted of the three hundred Hazaras, a squadron of cavalry, two mountain and two machine guns and some Rekis. The remnant of our original force and two machine guns were left in Khwash, under the command of Colonel Claridge.

The British officers with me were Major Sanders (Brigade Major), Major Lang, Captain Moore-Lane, Lieutenant Bream of the Hazaras, Lieutenant English with the guns, and Captain Brownlow in command of the cavalry. We started on a scorching hot day, the 28th of July, with Jiand's herds in the valley of the Sar-i-drokan as objective.

There were two ways of entering this valley, which is about seventy-five miles long, more or less closed at either end by a bottle-neck formation of hills, and protected along the whole length of its sides, as already described, by the precipitous Morpeish and Sar-i-drokan Ranges.

We fully realised that the entry to this valley would, in all probability, be a tough proposition, as the entrances could be easily defended, and would therefore be hard to force. The North-Western gorge, one of the two by which the valley could be entered, was called the Dast-Kird, and was very narrow. Jiand could, therefore, easily hold us in this direction. For, in an attack upon it, cavalry would only be an incumbrance, and, owing to the perpendicular sides of the gorge, and to the curious convexities of the hill-sides which obscured the view from below, the guns would fail in their proper sphere of usefulness.

Yet it would be necessary to enter the valley by that gorge, or by the alternative one at the South-Eastern end, and close to a place called Gusht. But this second gorge was almost as difficult of access, if defended, as that of the Dast-Kird.

It will be well to explain also that here, in the Sarhad, victory is attained more by the number of ramas—herds of goats and sheep—captured than by the number of men killed. It will be seen, therefore, that if we were to claim, and to be accredited with, a victory over Jiand, it became essential to capture the whole, or the greater part, of his herds.

This we well knew would be a difficult matter, but it would have to be done, despite Idu's doubts on the point.

" If you try to go in by the Dast-Kird, Sahib, Jiand will send his herds out by Gusht. If, on the other hand, you try to enter by Gusht, it will probably be fatal. Not only will Jiand send his herds out by the Dast-Kird, but as Gusht stands on the border of Halil Khan's territory he also will doubtless take you on, whilst it will only be a comparatively short distance for Jiand to make his dash through the Dast-Kird and so down to Khwash. While he is attacking the few men you have left in Khwash, you will be left at Gusht with Halil Khan guarding the defile! "

For once Idu had become a croaker, but we were not in the mood to listen to him.

We camped out in the open, but under the lea of the Morpeish Hills, and from out of those hills we knew that hundreds of eyes were watching our every movement.

At this stage I sent for Captain Brownlow and ordered him to march with the cavalry, while it was still light, for several miles in the direction of the Dast-Kird, at the same time making as big a display as he could; but, when night fell, to rejoin us as quickly and noiselessly as possible.

This little piece of strategy will be plain to the reader. When the enemy saw our cavalry, apparently going in the direction of the Dast-Kird, he would conclude that we intended to attack at that point. Jiand would, therefore, concentrate in that direction to defend the pass, and to prepare the ground for battle on the morrow. We, meantime, would be marching with all speed in the opposite direction—towards Gusht.

Accordingly, Captain Brownlow, making a fine show with his cavalry, set out towards the Dast-Kird, and continued in that direction till night-fall. But he went one better than his instructions. He found and collected a quantity of dried-up scrub, and this he set fire to in patches, to give the impression that our whole force was camping there on its way to the Dast-Kird. This done he returned to camp under cover of darkness.

Jiand fell into the trap. Warned by his scouts of what they imagined to be taking place he moved off with his force of something between one thousand and fifteen hundred fighting men, and actually marched all night towards the Dast-Kird. To safeguard his herds he sent them off in the opposite direction, towards Gusht. The position now amounted to this. Jiand's herds, on the farther side of the Morpeish Hills, and ourselves on the near side, were hurrying as fast as we could towards the Gusht defile, whilst Jiand and his men were hastening in the opposite direction—towards Dast-Kird. Thus it was that, by the time Jiand realised the trick that had been played upon him, we had gained a full two marches in the race for the defile.

Gusht—the town mentioned as being just outside the gorge of the same name—belonged to a Raider Chief with a name so difficult to pronounce that I never achieved it, and so was forced to call him "Gushti." The name has stuck to him I believe ever since. This Raider was at the head of about two hundred fighting men, and claimed to be a complete free lance, and to owe allegiance neither to Jiand, Halil Khan, nor anyone else. Gusht boasted a mud fort of some size, and from this stronghold "Gushti" raided at will.

I had been told that " Gushti " was prepared to join any force—as a free lance—if bent on an expedition which appealed to his taste. We were, in consequence, up against the fact that, if Jiand reached Gusht first, " Gushti " would undoubtedly be persuaded to join him. On the other hand, if we were first on the spot, it might be possible to bribe him into throwing in his lot with us.

The distance between Kamalabad, where we had first camped, and Gusht is about sixty miles, and the distance between Kamalabad and Dast-Kird is approximately fifteen miles. It will be understood, then, that while Jiand was marching the fifteen miles between Kamalabad and Dast-Kird we were moving fifteen miles in the opposite direction. When, therefore, he learned the truth as to the position, we were thirty miles ahead of him—a useful start. On learning his error Jiand turned and came hot-foot in pursuit of us along the farther slopes of the hills. And such good progress did he make, despite the difficulties of the ground, that he came very near to overtaking us, though, fortunately, not quite. The prize offered for the race was a big one, the unopposed passage of the Gusht defile, plus the active, or passive, assistance of " Gushti."

On the third day's march we approached, and deployed our force to give it as big a frontage as possible. This was done to impress " Gushti." As usual, we had sent messengers on ahead. These invited " Gushti " to join us, and pointed out the uselessness of opposition as Jiand was hopelessly behind, and promised large rewards if he decided to join us of his own free will.

When we arrived " Gushti " came out to meet us, all smiles and pleasantness, and assured me that he had not the slightest idea of opposing us, but that he would prefer not to fight against his old friend Halil Khan. He undoubtedly held him in wholesome dread. He also warned me that we were in for a big thing if we really meant fighting. Jiand might be behind, but not so very far, for, as usual, news of our proceedings had spread ahead of us. Jiand, he continued, with a very large force, was close on our heels, though on the other side of the range; whilst the Gamshadzais, under Halil Khan, were gathered in large numbers on the Southern slopes of the Safed-koh—about two marches away to the North of the Gusht defile—and were ready to attack us at any moment.

He admitted, however, that we had gained one great advantage, namely an unopposed passage through the defile.

We spent a very short time in Gusht, which boasted a considerable number of mud huts, as well as the fort already mentioned. There were also several karezes, and a fair number of date palms dotted about, which gave a picturesque appearance to the place. In addition, there was a spring which " Gushti " insisted on our seeing, and which was supposed to possess extraordinary qualities.

This spring gushes out of the top of a dome-shaped rock, and close beside it, also in the rock, is a hole called "The Hole of Judgment." If a man has been accused of wrongdoing, and is brought to this hole, a sure test of his innocence or guilt can be obtained. If, on thrusting his hand into the hole, he is able to draw it out again, he is innocent. If he cannot perform the feat he is guilty. This appears to be an unfailing method of obtaining absolution for their sins.

We passed through the defile that evening, though we had already had a long march, for I did not want to risk losing the advantage we had gained. Once through the neck we debouched into comparatively open ground, and, after continuing our march for some three miles, halted and encamped by the side of a fine kareze.

That same night Jiand arrived at a point only five miles distant. We had not, therefore, won the race with much to spare. Later information showed that he had travelled night and day, and was deeply depressed to find that, owing to his initial mistake, we had passed, unopposed, what should have been a formidable barrier.

The next morning we advanced about three miles along the valley, subject to a certain amount of sniping which grew worse as we proceeded. We encamped in a strong position by a spring. We were fully aware that, at any moment, the Yarmahom-medzais in front of us might join hands with the

Gamshadzais. Their combined forces would then number anything between two thousand to two thousand five hundred men.

We now learned that a large number of the Gamshadzai herds had been sent to a place called Makn-tuk in the Safed-koh hills beyond the Saragan defile. I decided to attack in the direction of Makn-tuk.

Accordingly, at about five o'clock on the following morning, we attacked the Gamshadzais' position by the Saragan defile, but at the outset the opposition proved far greater than we had anticipated, and, though this attack was pushed till eleven o'clock, the main body had then only advanced about half a mile.

I then realised that it would be futile to hope to push on to Makn-tuk, and, much against my will, withdrew the scattered forces, some of which were already engaged far up on the hill-sides. With the help of covering fire from the Maxim and mountain guns, we withdrew with comparatively small loss to our last camping ground.

The Hazaras were very disappointed at this order to retire, for they declared that, had they been allowed to advance, they would, most certainly, have succeeded in knocking out the opposition and winning through to Makn-tuk. But during our passage through that region at a later date these fire-eaters were better able to gauge the extraordinary difficulty of the terrain, and had to admit that it would have been impossible to fight a way through.

In the meantime a body of the enemy had moved down from the hills, and had cut off our only available water supply by capturing the picket-post guarding the spring before mentioned.

This was serious and I immediately rode forward with an escort of about a dozen cavalrymen. But we had not proceeded far when, quite suddenly, a heavy fire was opened on us from the hills. Fortunately no one was hit, but it was a miraculous escape, for the ground around us was literally ploughed up with bullets.

We dismounted, attacked and regained the picket-post. As Brownlow and I entered the sangar I noticed, on the ground at my feet, one of my own cigarette boxes, which had been taken by the Raiders when they captured my kit on its way from Nushki to Robat.

The dozen Sawars were now left to defend the spring, at any cost, and Brownlow and I returned to the main body, meeting on the way the Sarhad-dar, with some of the Rekis, who were coming to our assistance. However, the danger was over for the moment.

The Rekis solemnly assured me that I must be tir-band (immune from fire). They had watched the hail of bullets from the hills spattering around us, and could yet hardly believe we had none of us been hit.

I had already found by experience that it was always wise to take advantage of little superstitious suggestions of this sort, so solemnly replied that it was a well-known fact that I was tir-band!

We had now seen enough of the enemy's ways and methods to realise his inclination to waste a great deal of invaluable ammunition at long ranges. We, therefore, decided upon what seemed a wise course of action. Realising that to attack him in the hills would be too expensive we would remain down in the open, anyhow for a few days, draw his fire, and give him a good opportunity of eating up his limited food supply. We had food for a month, and knew that he had only sufficient to last four or five days.

Accordingly we camped where we were for that night, and on the following morning moved a little farther back towards the Gusht gorge, taking up the position upon which we had camped when first entering the valley.

On that short rearward march we were fired at continuously, first at long range, and then, as the enemy grew bolder, at close quarters. We could distinctly hear them shouting as they came, crouching low amongst the rocks and scrub of the hill-sides. They were humorists, too, these Sarhadis, for, between the shouts, we could catch a very passable imitation of the rat-a-tat-tat noise of our machine guns. They came, at last, near enough to shout at me, directly and personally, calling on me to surrender; promising if I did so to spare my life, and also informing me that it was no good trying to fight any longer as I was practically surrounded, and my retreat cut off. They used the selfsame expressions I had so often used when summoning them to surrender. This was turning the tables with a vengeance! But we quickly saw that their boast as to having cut our retreat was not altogether an idle one. They had, at this stage, actually occupied a little mud fort crowning a small hillock. This hillock lay like an island in the bottom of the valley, and commanded the camping ground we were making for.

The Raiders could be plainly seen shooting at us through the loop-holes, but, unfortunately for them, Lieutenant English promptly trained one of his mountain guns on the fort. The first round fired hit its mark, burst inside, and raised a huge cloud of dust. Its disconcerted occupants promptly bolted, and the way to our camping ground lay open.

Here it was possible to place the whole force in comparative safety, partly owing to the cover afforded by the hillock with the mud fort on its summit, and in a greater measure to the very convex slopes of the hills to the North, which gave us complete shelter from snipers' bullets.

Our only vulnerable point was from behind. If the enemy collected in the low hills running out from the sides of the gorge it would be possible to rush us in the darkness. It was in that direction, accordingly, that we must look out for trouble.

With the idea of guarding against this I asked " Gushti " to supply me with a couple of men who knew the country well, and were able to find their way amongst the hills by night.

I then waited till it was quite dark before sending out two strong pickets, each consisting of fifty men, under the guidance of "Gushti's" men, to occupy two of the low hills which Sanders and I had carefully noted whilst the daylight lasted. These commanded the ground over which the attack would most likely come. We now fully realised that we were in a very tight corner, and that there was nothing to be done but to stay and fight it out.

That night Halil Khan himself arrived with reinforcements from Jalk, and went straight to Jiand and his Yarmahommedzais.

He harangued them on their lack of enterprise in not having already defeated my force and made me a prisoner. He told the tribesmen that they vastly outnumbered my men and suggested that, if Jiand had lost his nerve, they had better serve, for the time being, under his leadership, when they would soon see how to capture the Sahib's forces. The outcome of this forceful personality's action was that Jiand, old and now very weary, consented to waive his leadership in Halil Khan's favour—for the time being.

So sure seems Halil Khan to have been of his ultimate and complete victory over us on the morrow that he actually sent a messenger off, that night, to the Khan of Bampur, telling him that the British General, who had caused so much trouble, was

HAZARAS ON A PICKET POST BELOW WHICH HALIL KHAN WAS KILLED.

already a captive, and that hundreds of his men had been killed. He also wound up this premature message by inviting the Khan to come and share the loot.

He then left Jiand's camp, taking with him Jiand's men, marched right round our position to our rear, and occupied a long, deep hollow between the two very low hills on which the pickets had been posted, but whose presence was absolutely unsuspected, as they had got there noiselessly in the darkness.

From this hollow an easy advance on our camp could be made, and Halil Khan's intention had been, with the dawn, to rush us, and by sheer weight of numbers, overwhelm us.

But just before dawn one of those insignificant accidents occurred upon which great things so often depend.

As Halil Khan made ready for the attack, which I heard later was timed to take place during the next ten minutes, the rifle of one of his men went off by accident.

I distinctly heard the shot, and have since been told that I rushed out of my tent shouting, " The Lord has delivered them into our hands! "

I am perfectly certain I never said any such thing, though I may have exclaimed, " We've got em! "

In an instant a roar of musketry broke out from the hills on both sides, for the shot had alarmed the pickets, and they were firing down into the hollow from whence the sound had come.

Light was beginning to break, and it was then just sufficient to see by, dimly and uncertainly. In any case I knew I had got my chance.

Instant orders were given that every man in camp should reinforce the pickets.

It soon became apparent that Halil Khan, ignorant that the heights above him were occupied, had committed a grave error. Daylight showed that his force were completely exposed to our fire, and that he could neither advance nor retire without running the gauntlet of it; for this grew hotter and hotter as reinforcements came up.

Halil Khan and his men fought like tigers, but were in an impossible position. We had all the ammunition we required and an easy target. Our own casualties were astonishingly light, but we did not get off scot-free, and Halil Khan was personally responsible for many of our men.

By eleven o'clock the fight was over, and those of the enemy remaining alive got clear as best they could.

Before long news was brought that Halil Khan had been killed, and that his body was still lying in the hollow. Immediate orders were given for it to be brought in, as I feared the Shiah Hazaras might attempt to mutilate it. One of the Hazaras spread the news that he had seen me blow Halil Khan's head off. The Sarhad-dar overheard him, repeated what the Hazara had said, and asked me to go and look at the body, which had now been brought in.

A number of us went and looked at the body, and found that a bullet had pierced his eye and had blown the back of his head off.

One of the Rekis, who had been present at the last Durbar in Khwash, exclaimed, " Sahib, you are a Buzurg (a prophet). You said at the Durbar in Khwash that if ever Halil Khan fought against you again you would blow his head off. And behold, you have done it."

Once again I felt it policy to acquiesce and to admit that I was a prophet. As a fact, I had not fired a single shot during the engagement.

Soon after I had returned to my tent an irate, native officer of the Hazaras craved admission, which was accorded. Without preface he opened bluntly. " Sahib, will you give us Halil Khan's body? "

I asked, " Why? What do you mean to do with it? Do you want to mutilate it? "

He replied, " Sahib, when we lost men the day before yesterday, and buried them before retiring, the Yarmahommedzais, who came down after our departure, dug up the bodies, mutilated them horribly and flung them to the jackals. Therefore, in justice, Halil Khan's body is ours."

" Halil Khan was a brave man as well as a great leader," I replied. " You are going to give him a soldier's funeral. You surely have no wish to treat him in the same terrible way that your men were treated? "

He urged his point of view with such heat that I

at last grew angry and asked him by what right he demanded Halil Khan's body, and to answer me as to who had killed him.

"You did, Sahib," he replied, eyeing me curiously.

"Exactly," I said with decision. "Then to whom does the body belong—to you or to me?"

This seemed rather to appeal to him, for he replied with greater calm:

"To you, Sahib, I suppose."

"I suppose so too, and I am going to do what I like with it. Go at once to Gusht, buy a new winding sheet, and we will give Halil Khan a soldier's burial; one befitting his brave deeds and position. Bring in all the mullahs (priests) you can find in Gusht. Oh, and, by the way, you can pay for the winding sheet for wasting so much of my time in argument."

So we accorded Halil Khan a really fine soldier's funeral. Nor was this without results, for we learned, later, that it had made a great and favourable impression throughout the Sarhad.

CHAPTER XII

VICTORY AND PEACE

News of the herds—Towards Dast-Kird—Water!—Mutton for all—Dast-Kird—A stampede—Back to Khwash—On the track of the Gamshadzais—Twice a prophet—The Sharhaddar's roost—Before Jalk—Rejected terms—More strategy and a bloodless victory—Remain only terms and sick leave.

WE had certainly won a decisive victory from a military point of view, but, according to the unwritten code regulating victory in the Sarhad, we had yet to capture the Raiders' *ramas* or herds of goats and sheep.

This omission still confronted us when one of Idu's special Reki scout declared he knew the exact whereabouts of Jiand's herds, and that he could lead us there in two marches. At the end of each of these he declared we should also find a good camping ground, and a good water supply. As these men had never yet promised water and failed us, orders were given to strike camp and march out in the direction of Dast-Kird, through the valley lying between the Morpeish and Sar-i-drokan Ranges.

Although we made a very early start the heat soon became intense. There was not a particle of shade, and our route lay slightly uphill all the way, over rugged broken ground. Also, as we were confident of finding water at the camping ground, the men had emptied their water bottles before mid-day, and were enduring agonies of thirst long before we reached our proposed camping place; whilst the suffering of the animals was pitiful to see. But the prospect of a good drink at the end of the march kept up our spirits.

At last, late in the afternoon, the Reki, who had constituted himself our guide, gave a cry and ran forward, telling us that we had reached the spot where we should find water.

No sign of stream or spring showed itself, but I remembered that the Sarhadis have a way of finding water seemingly miraculous to the white man, and when the Reki proceeded to dig and scratch in the ground at the foot of a stunted tree we fully expected to see a little spring gush forth. The men, therefore, with lips swollen and tongues cleaving to the roofs of their mouths, crowded round, eager and impatient.

But, for once, Nature and the Reki failed us. For though the latter dug and dug, with the sweat pouring down his face, the dry, arid ground showed not the faintest sign of moisture.

At last he desisted and fell at my feet, saying despairingly, "Sahib, there is no water! I found water here once, in the cold season, and I thought it would always be here. The heat must have dried it all up."

Our situation was pretty desperate. We had not a drop of water for man or beast, and now could not

WATER! ON THE MARCH TO THE SAR-I-DROKAN.

tell when we should get any. All through the latter part of that day's march we had succeeded in getting the men along solely by encouraging them with promises of water. "Just a mile farther on" and then, "perhaps another half-mile." Only those who have marched without water in torrid countries can have any conception of the depression that grips men when they do not know when, or where, water may next be found.

I cursed the man for misleading us, and he shook with fear. "It is not my fault, Sahib. Water was here when last I came to this place. But to-morrow, without fail, I will lead you to a fine stream of water."

"To-morrow?" I echoed. "How are we to exist till to-morrow? Why should I believe you? You have deceived us to-day, why not again to-morrow?"

The man swore on the Koran he could and would lead us to a place where we should find water. "If I do not succeed, Sahib, in finding water before eleven o'clock, then take my life."

I replied grimly that if he failed again, his life would most certainly be forfeit—that was to say if any of us then remained in a condition to shoot him.

The whole force suffered horribly that night, and when we set out again it was still dark. The Reki went on ahead with the advance guard. I rather imagine he was anxious to put a safe distance between himself and my revolver, for I had, indeed, determined to have him shot if he deceived us a second time. No man could face a second day of that blinding heat and glare without water and keep his sanity.

We had only been marching a few hours when a Sawar rode back from the advance guard to report that large herds of sheep and goats had been sighted a short distance ahead.

Our spirits instantly rose. Where there were sheep there would, most probably, be water. Shouting to the men to encourage them we galloped forward and were soon pushing our way through masses of sheep to find ourselves on the banks of a stream of clear, cool water.

The difficulty, of course, was now to restrain man and beast from over-drinking; for if ever nectar flowed on this earth it flowed that day in that parched, sun-baked Saragan Valley.

Unfortunately, like the majority of streams in the Sarhad, and in Persia generally, it only flowed above ground for a short distance, to be soon lost again in the arid, sandy ground. So orders were given to halt at that spot till we were all rested, and had absorbed sufficient water to make up for the past thirty-six hours.

The thirty-four herds of sheep and goats found here were claimed as spoils of war, and I determined to give the men a real, good feast for once. Here was any amount of mutton for the killing, and well-nigh as much goats' milk as water.

The hungry Hazaras sent in a request that they might each have a whole sheep a day. I naturally thought such a request fantastic, and, not taking it literally, sent back word that they might, for once, have as much meat as they wanted.

But they took the permission literally, and actually did slaughter a sheep for each man. I discovered afterwards that their great idea had been to be able to boast, in the future, that, after their great victory over the Yarmahommedzais, led by the Gamshadzai Chief, Halil Khan, their rations had been "a sheep per man per day."

After this feast the carcasses of the uneaten sheep, and of the half-cooked meat, lay about in an orgy of waste, and the sight of the camping-ground was, as may be imagined, a sickening one. Never again was such a ration-order given!

Late in the afternoon, with the whole force in fine fettle, we continued our forward march, driving the herds with us, and, a little later, found a good camping ground with a plentiful supply of water. For many hours that night, owing to the bleating of thousands of sheep, there was little rest for anyone. But as they were now *our* sheep and not the enemy's, the annoyance was cheerfully borne.

Upon the following day water proved scarce, and a great deal of digging had to be done before even a trickle could be found. The unfortunate sheep and animals had, therefore, to go very short. The country was also from this point getting very difficult, and marching became a great labour in consequence. Part of our route lay through a narrow, rocky defile; one of the worst to negotiate, from a military point of view, that I have ever encountered. Had a mere handful of the enemy chosen to obstruct us it would have been utterly impossible to get through.

Much picketing of the heights had to be done, and this called for a great effort on the part of the Hazara Pioneers. These duties were well carried out under the very able direction of Major Lang.

Fortunately the Yarmahommedzais had had enough of it, and left us severely alone. In fact, the only signs we had of them were the blood tracks of their wounded, walking or carried. But even these were significant enough evidence of their losses during the fight.

The next day brought us more open ground, though marching still remained arduous, as we were tackling an uphill route. But later it fell away again towards the Dast-Kird gorge, and, by the afternoon, we were able to pitch our camp in a wild, but very picturesque, little valley, close to Jiand's Summer haunt. This valley, as I have already explained, lies between the Morpeish and Sar-i-drokan heights, which at this point rise sheer from it on either side. There are also a good many trees in the neighbourhood, and the ground round the bases of these had been flattened, and then plastered with mud, in order to form good flooring for jugis.

We spent the night here, and on the following day arrived at Dast-Kird, where we camped close to a small stream. Unfortunately this stream was so small, a mere trickle, that it would not suffice for the animals, who had had insufficient water for the last two or three days.

These herds were some little distance behind, for, poor brutes, they were feeling the heat and lack of water terribly. We, therefore, proceeded to make some provision for them, before their arrival, by damming the stream, and trying to make a small reservoir.

The first animals to arrive were the battery mules, who, when they smelt water, made a dash for it. But they had scarcely begun to drink than a mass of twelve thousand sheep and goats, also smelling water, broke from their would-be shepherds, and, in a solid phalanx, charged the mules, routed them, and took possession of the water-supply. The men pulled and tugged, and struck them with their rifles in their endeavour to stampede them and drink themselves. But those sheep knew the power of numbers and of combination. With their heads well down they slaked their thirst from a stream which, now that the dam had been trodden down, had again become a trickle, and they held that position, against all comers, for twenty minutes. Poor beasts, they paid for their orgy at the price of some two hundred lives that night.

Upon the following day we started on our return

march to Khwash, and, upon our entry there, were accorded a great reception, and the story of the fight had to be told again and again.

It was during this march that we began to realise the extent of the Yarmahommedzai casualties in the recent fighting; for, during the whole of it, from the scene of the fight right through to Khwash, a distance of about a hundred miles, not a single one of the enemy did we see, nor was a solitary shot fired at us.

But I was still not quite satisfied with results. We had not yet closely engaged and beaten the Gamshadzais, nor had we put into operation that deciding factor, the capture of their herds. On the contrary, when we had attempted to pierce the Saragan defile, they had forced us to retire.

I have never yet been able to understand why Halil Khan never brought his own force against us near Gusht, but only the Yarmahommedzais, after he had persuaded Jiand to let him lead the latter into battle.

It can only be supposed that he thought he had a task easy enough to tackle with one lashkar, and that he would not, in consequence, endanger his own men's lives. The mystery is the deeper because he had previously been at great pains to collect all his scattered tribesmen, and had concentrated them in the Safed-koh. Yet these men, even when news reached them of our victory over Jiand's tribe and of the death of their leader, never made the smallest attempt to attack us or to reverse the decision of arms.

It will be understood, then, that while the Gamshadzais remained unbeaten and their herds intact, our claim to dominance in the Sarhad could not be claimed as anything but partial. If, therefore, we were to hope for lasting peace in the future, they too must have a lesson.

So, after a couple of days' rest at Khwash, we marched out with our faces once more turned towards Gusht, and with every hope of another victory. The composition of the force was much the same as that upon the previous occasion, but with the addition of a few Chagai Levies under Major Hutchinson (political officer).

A couple of days' marching across the burning plain found us camped at a place called Ab-i-kahugan, lying in a small valley closely surrounded by hills. The men were hot and weary, and, as water had been scarce on the march, they were only too thankful to fling themselves down and rest. There were a small water hole and a few stunted trees and shrubs under which a certain amount of shade could be obtained.

For myself I dropped down under one of these bushes and slept well on into the afternoon. When at last I woke, still feeling very done up with the heat, I saw one or two flashes of lightning in the distance, and felt certain that it was going to rain.

I immediately got up and gave orders for the

whole camp to be moved on to higher ground, and selected a likely spot on one of the slopes of the low hills surrounding the valley.

The heat was still very great, and the effort expended in striking and re-pitching camp was not inconsiderable. The present camping-place was also infinitely cooler and more comfortable.

As an outcome of this order an officer reported that the men were grumbling at having to move when tired out with the heat and the heavy marching of the last few days.

I explained (for I knew by my own state how tired and done the men must be) that I had a presentiment that it was going to rain and that, if it did, the dry valley-bed would soon be a running stream.

The officer stared at me. "Rain?" he repeated, as though he had not heard me aright. "But it hardly ever rains in the Sarhad, and it has never been known to rain in August."

"Nevertheless," I replied, "this valley-bottom is going to be turned upside down, and the sooner you get your men out of it and up on to high ground the better."

The officer saluted and returned to his men, who sulkily proceeded to carry up their kit and tents and to form a new camp on the uncomfortable, sloping sides of the hill.

As I strolled about, seeing that my orders were being carried out, I noticed that Major Hutchinson's tent had been left in the bed of the valley. I walked up to it, found him dozing inside, and told him to have his tent moved on to higher ground as it was going to rain.

He, however, demurred, saying that he was very tired. He added, " It never rains in the month of August in Baluchistan."

I, however, remained firm, though the few light clouds flecking the sky a short while before had completely disappeared.

Despite my stringent orders some of Major Hutchinson's Chagai Levies apparently passed unnoticed amongst the low scrub, and so remained down in the shady comfort of the valley.

As the evening wore on I began to feel that perhaps I had been foolish in ignoring the dogmatic statements of the men well acquainted with weather conditions in the Sarhad, and was still chewing the cud of this reflection when, suddenly, I heard a roar in the distance. This came rapidly nearer, and very quickly resolved itself into the sound of rushing water. Almost before we realised it, a mighty spate swept into the valley, literally filling it. The water carried everything before it, and very soon small trees, shrubs and débris were being hurled along in a mighty rush.

It was pretty evident that the rain foretold had indeed fallen, though actually, in another part of the hills, forming this spate, which would have caused us serious loss but for my lucky premonition.

Torrents of rain accompanied the spate, and

the kit of the few Chagai Levies who had neglected orders was carried away and never seen again.

As for the Levies themselves, they came within an ace of losing their own lives, and only saved themselves by clambering into the branches of some stunted trees, and waiting there till rescued. Nor was the rescue-work done without considerable risk to the rescuers.

The Sarhad-dar had, for some reason, been down in the valley-bed when the spate arrived, and had been nearly drawn under during the first few minutes. But he too, fortunately, managed to climb into a low tree, where for some time his position was perilous enough, for the swirling waters threatened every minute to snap or uproot the trunk, when he would have been carried away.

It was pitch dark when the spate arrived. I had seized a hurricane lamp from my tent and was watching the amazing scene by its light, when I heard the Sarhad-dar's voice shouting for help. One of our resourceful Rekis instantly grasped the situation. He jumped on to one of the horses tethered close by, urged him into the flood, and soon had the Sarhad-dar safely beside me on the high ground. He was later on recommended for the Royal Humane Society's Medal.

The next morning, as soon as I was awake, my tent was besieged by the Hazaras. They crowded round, asking me to come out. So slipping into my kit I emerged with the intention of asking them what they wanted.

But I had scarcely lifted the tent-flap when they all raised a shout, and then proceeded to tell me that I was a Buzurg (prophet), that they all owed their lives to me, and had come to thank me.

I replied with proper solemnity. It was undeniable, I said, that I was a prophet, for had they not recently had two concrete instances of my powers?

Later on, Major Hutchinson, in thanking me for saving his life, asked: " How did you know it was going to rain? "

I laughingly replied, " Because I'm a prophet, my son! Didn't you hear the Hazaras proclaim it just now? "

As a matter of fact we had very great reason to be thankful for our escape. The loss of the whole of our camp equipment, and of hundreds of our animals, would have been inevitable had the camp remained on its original site.

The day following this incident we marched through Gusht again, and camped on the site of our recent engagement.

From here we resumed our march in the direction of Zaiti, a camping ground lying just beyond the Saragan defile. But though we started at five a.m., met with no opposition and reckoned the distance only about twelve miles, we were not through the defile before midnight.

It must have been at about this hour that I called

one of the native Hazara officers to my side, and remarked, " Your men were very disappointed the other day when we tried to force the pass, and the order was given to retire. You remember, they said they were convinced they could have got through, even with the heavy opposition we encountered. Do you think, now they've seen what it's really like, they are satisfied that the order was a necessary one? "

" Sahib," he replied, " of course we all see now that we could have done nothing in such a place against a determined enemy. I have never been through such a place in my life, and I am used to rough and difficult country."

As a matter of fact the defile was so narrow in places that a loaded camel could not get through it. Fortunately we had a quantity of gun cotton with us, so were able to blast the rocks here and there, and thus make the passage possible for them without unloading.

In due course we arrived at the village of Sinukan, a place some eleven miles from Jalk. Jalk at the time was a Gamshadzai stronghold, where they held two forts of some strength.

At Sinukan I received a message from the Gamshadzais saying that they wished to treat with me, and asking whether I would go into Jalk and state my terms. If these were acceptable, they said, they would instantly submit, but, if not, they undertook to withdraw their forces to a distance of five miles on

HAZARA PIONEERS WIDENING A PASSAGE FOR LOADED CAMELS.

the farther side of Jalk, provided we also withdrew five miles from the town on our side. This suggestion was made in order to give us both time to make our respective dispositions before fighting commenced.

An answer was sent to say that I agreed to the conditions, and that my force would come at once into Jalk to meet the Chiefs and present my terms to them.

I would say here that these terms were not drastic. They were only bare necessary safeguards for the lasting peace of the Sarhad. On their presentation, therefore, and for a time during the discussion, I hoped that counsels of wisdom would prevail, and that they would be accepted *in toto*. At the last minute, however, the hotheads over-ruled the moderates and they were formally rejected.

On this rejection I warned them that, if they persisted in their refusal, it meant fighting, and their reply was that they fully recognised the gravity of their decision, but that they meant to abide by it.

Accordingly, we retired not only five miles but the whole eleven miles back to Sinukan. My reason for this action was that I had already thought out a plan by which it might be possible to subdue these warlike tribesmen without the fighting I was naturally anxious to avoid. I certainly did not want to lose my own men, nor did I wish to make casualties of any more of the Sarhadis. My chief object had been, throughout, and, as has already been mentioned in this narrative, to make friends with them in the long run.

But no race, white or coloured, ever held in respect man or government showing weakness or indecision, and, as the foregoing pages prove, it was of little use attempting to make friends with these tribesmen without first inspiring them with a wholesome respect for British arms.

As we approached Sinukan I directed my Brigade Major to form two separate camps as I wished to seize Jalk by surprise that night with a portion of my force. My idea was to leave my transport and other encumbrances under a sufficient guard at Sinukan and with the remainder to move off secretly to carry out my intentions. Great care was taken to keep my idea secret, and only a few officers knew my intention. So well was the secret kept that my personal servant, Allah-dad, brought me my tea next morning only to find my bed empty.

At midnight, very quietly we roused the troops and marched off. Before dawn we arrived outside the town. It was only at the very last moment that the Gamshadzais, who had learned that I had gone straight back to Sinukan, and, in consequence, had not anticipated an attack that night, got wind of our approach. They were, therefore, taken completely by surprise, and utterly lost their heads. As we charged into the place with the cavalry they all took to their heels and rushed out on the other side,

CHAHQIRD FORT IN JALK.

leaving many arms behind them. Within a very few minutes the two forts were in our hands.

My men soon rounded up the few Gamshadzais who had remained in the place, which seemed otherwise to be full of women and children.

To my embarrassment three large *ramas* of weeping women and children were presently led up to where I was sitting under a tree on the bank of a stream. I was then informed that they were all mine.

Some of them, in tears, asked me what I was going to do with them.

I replied, " I don't know. But at any rate I am English and not a German. What would you like me to do with you? "

They seemed bewildered at first, and without understanding, but when I assured them that I was speaking seriously, and really wanted to know what they would like to do, they soon found their tongues and made known the fact that they would like to go to their own homes.

" Is that all? " I replied. " Well then, go."

Their faces which, at first, shone with joy soon fell again. " But, Sahib, we have nothing left. You have captured all our possessions."

" But I don't want them," I returned. " Take everything that is yours and go."

Their thanks were then overwhelming, but I cut them short. " Wait a bit before you thank me so much. No Englishman ever makes war against woman and children—but there are your men. If I catch them, after all the trouble they've given me, I shall certainly kill them."

"Kill them then, Sahib," they said scornfully. "They deserted us, and ran away, when you and your lashkar came in. It is all they deserve."

As a matter of fact I learned, soon afterwards, that the Gamshadzais had not only run out of Jalk, but right out of the Sarhad, to take refuge in other districts. By thus evacuating their own country they acknowledged their final defeat.

It is reasonable to suppose that this humiliating end to their opposition would never have occurred had Halil Khan been alive. He, at least, would have been game to the last. He would have died fighting at Jalk—as he had indeed died at Gusht—or he would have surrendered with dignity. Halil Khan was a fine man, and without his leadership the spirit of his men at first faltered and then failed.

It seemed then that, by this last action with the Gamshadzais, the prestige of the British had been completely restored throughout the Sarhad. In the West, Juma Khan, leader of the Ismailzais, had faithfully kept his word to, and had demonstrated his friendship and loyalty for, the British cause, ever since he had pledged both at Kacha. In the centre of the district the Yarmahommedzais had been completely defeated in open action. In the East the Gamshadzais had abandoned their arms and had bolted from the country.

There was now nothing left to be done.

We, therefore, returned, marching easily to Khwash, where, very shortly after our arrival, I received letters from both the Yarmahommedzais and Gamshadzais asking to be allowed to return to their respective homes in the Sarhad, and on any terms that might be imposed.

I had had eight months of continual work in the hot weather of the Sarhad and was very near the end of my tether. As a fact I was, by that time, suffering badly in health in many ways, and our medical officer insisted upon an immediate return to India for a long rest.

As the Sarhad was now completely ours, and as it only remained for the political officers to dictate terms to the tribes, I listened to the advice of that medical officer, applied for leave to return to Simla, and was, in due course, granted it.

But, though the need for rest in a cooler climate was urgent, it was with real regret that I said good-bye to Khwash, the centre of so many hopes and fears, and the scene of such dramatic happenings.

INDEX

PRINTED IN GREAT BRITAIN BY
THE NORTHUMBERLAND PRESS, LIMITED
WATERLOO HOUSE, THORNTON STREET
NEWCASTLE-UPON-TYNE

THE RAIDERS OF THE SARHAD